Drama Queens

DRAMA QUEENS
Vickie Gendreau

Translated by Aimee Wall

LITERATURE IN TRANSLATION SERIES
BOOK*HUG PRESS 2019

FIRST ENGLISH EDITION

Published originally under the title: *Drama Queens* © 2014 by Le Quartanier
Published with permission of Le Quartanier
English translation copyright © 2019 by Aimee Wall

LIBRARY AND ARCHIVES CANADA CATALOGUING IN PUBLICATION

Title: Drama queens / Vickie Gendreau ; translated by Aimee Wall.
Other titles: Drama queens. English
Names: Gendreau, Vickie, author. | Wall, Aimee, translator.
Description: First English edition. | Series statement: Literature in translation series
Series: Literature in translation series.
Originally published in French under the title: Drama queens.

Identifiers: Canadiana (print) 20190192356 | Canadiana (ebook) 20190192364
ISBN 9781771665223 (softcover) | ISBN 9781771665230 (HTML)
ISBN 9781771665247 (PDF) | ISBN 9781771665254 (Kindle)

Classification: LCC PS8613.E535 D7313 2019 | DDC C843/.6—dc23

PRINTED IN CANADA

The production of this book was made possible through the generous assistance of the Canada Council for the Arts and the Ontario Arts Council. Book*hug Press also acknowledges the support of the Government of Canada through the Canada Book Fund and the Government of Ontario through the Ontario Book Publishing Tax Credit and the Ontario Book Fund.

We acknowledge the financial support of the Government of Canada through the National Translation Program for Book Publishing, an initiative of the *Roadmap for Canada's Official Languages 2013-2018: Education, Immigration, Communities*, for our translation activities.

Book*hug Press acknowledges that the land on which we operate is the traditional territory of many nations, including the Mississaugas of the Credit, the Anishnabeg, the Chippewa, the Haudenosaunee and the Wendat peoples. We recognize the enduring presence of many diverse First Nations, Inuit and Métis peoples and are grateful for the opportunity to meet and work on this territory.

Introduction

In the winter of 2013, Vickie Gendreau's tumour returned after barely five months of remission, during which she had published *Testament*, been recognized as a real writer, and become a celebrity of the small literary world of Quebec. She had also continued writing. The doctors decided on a particularly gruelling chemotherapy treatment for the relapse, and by early March, the treatments and the constant doses of cortisone had left Vickie extremely weak. I went to see her one afternoon, and we talked about how little time she likely had left, given the diagnosis. She told me that her biggest wish before dying was to hold the book she was working on in her hands. She said she couldn't finish the manuscript—the fatigue was too intense and her morale too low. I told her I could take what she'd written up to that point and contact Éric de Larochellière, the managing editor at Le Quartanier, to see if it would be possible to put together and print a single copy. I left her place with a set of documents on a USB key. When I arrived home, I got in touch with de Larochellière to ask what would be possible. He said that, apart from the cover, which could only be printed in large print runs, the single copy would be identical to other Le Quartanier books—the layout, the size, the paper. He told me to come by the next day with the documents.

The documents Vickie had given me didn't read like a coherent novel. I did what I could to construct one from them, without writing or rewriting anything. I worked almost non-stop for eighteen hours. The manuscript I put together worked, and I was able to get it to Le Quartanier's offices on time.

In the days that followed, Vickie finished her chemo treatments and her health improved a little. I went over to her place one afternoon with a printed copy of the manuscript I'd put together. I was worried my work didn't reflect her intentions for the book, and so we ended up reading it together page by page.

A week or two later, she underwent another round of tests. The treatment hadn't worked. There was nothing left to do, and there was very little time. Vickie, who never wrote better than when she was in the midst of an intense ordeal, picked back up the work I'd done, reclaimed the structure I'd created, and wrote new passages. The team at Le Quartanier and the printer worked quickly, and the single copy arrived in time. She cried with joy when she first held it. We had a little party. But that wasn't enough for her; she wanted to give a public reading of the book. Her friends threw all their energy into the project, and the public reading of *Drama Queens* took place in a packed theatre in Montreal one Tuesday afternoon. A hundred and fifty people listened for five hours to the entire text of the novel, which they were hearing for the first time. It was the most intense event I've ever attended. The audience listened in silence, they laughed, they started sobbing at the end. The text spoke of events that had occurred, in some cases, just the week before, recounted in a style that made us feel that the book would outlive us all. We were at a literary funeral in the presence of the author. Everyone knew it and nobody wanted to admit it.

The public reading of *Drama Queens* took place on April 30, 2013. On May 4, Vickie Gendreau went into palliative care. She died on May 11.

The book published as *Drama Queens* is essentially Vickie's final text, the one read in public. While *Testament* recounts the experience of illness, but speaks of death in the realm of fantasy, *Drama Queens* recounts the experience of impending death, and life becomes the fantasy—the life of a double, a sister invented for the book. Vickie had wanted to write a book about the intensity of life, to continue living out her partying twenties vicariously through this novel. But at a certain point, the stage curtain is ripped down, the backdrop crumbles, and we see the sickness lurking in the wings, in all its ugliness: the anxiety, the deformed body, the walker, the wheelchair, the diapers. Everything we'd hidden, she and I, those afternoons at her place, everything we'd hidden so we could keep making sure life had the upper hand on death, she wrote it all, hiding nothing. That refusal to hide anything, ever—it was this that would make *Drama Queens* a great book, and Vickie Gendreau a great writer.

—*Mathieu Arsenault*

PART ONE

ANNA KETAMINE, VICTORIA LOVE
and MAGGIE BOOKS
invite you to their first group exhibition.

VICTORIA LOVE, *Artistic Director*

Welcome to our first group exhibition. I'm working in visual arts now. Literature too. I should hurry and finish my text before my head starts spinning. Thankfully, once it's printed, it's done. I'll decorate it with a few gemstones. The pleasures of a hot glue gun. Everyone contributes their little something. Anna Ketamine is doing performance art and installations. Maggie Books made these little cinematographic fantasies, and I printed out all my notebooks. I sit in my wheelchair in the middle of the museum. I invite everyone to read the pile in front of me. Men in particular. I'm still hoping for a Prince Charming. My king. For the more visual types, there's the exhibition. I make out, I die, I do it all.

They prescribed me fiction. They said it could be good for me. I hide my pill organizer behind my computer. My breakfast is brought to me in bed. On a silver platter. I'd be there, all sexy in a negligee. I should demand tropical fruits. There should be sun filling the room through expensive curtains. There should be. There should always be something more.

Life runs fast, and death catches up. Life is an elaborate exhibition, and death a play. I'm going to be very sincere in these notebooks. I'm going to reveal it all to you. Give you clues through my work. I'll even try fiction so you can escape from your daily life too. I'll talk about Facebook, Google, relationships, this infamous generation. More illness, more fennec foxes.

You enter the room. The hangar, really. You say: "These girls must have cash. These pieces are enormous. All the characters are wearing precious gems. Or, anyway, you can't tell if they're fake." Nothing is really that beautiful. It is not a question of should, but must.

They're going to freeze me like Walt Disney once they see our exhibition. Francis asked me to spit in my first book instead of signing it. They'll be able to clone me like that goat. The book is dead. Long live the book.

We spend so much time thinking about how to decorate our carcasses. A necklace, a jacket. A dress with precious gems around the neck. A little scarf, a pair of earrings. Vintage. Everything vintage. Then we die. It's over. What to wear in my coffin? I want an urn with a little crown. No. I am not a robot. Yes. I'd like the robot's life. When I put my Dollar Max crown on the little fountain they never turn on, it looks like Wall-E's girlfriend. I want to be Wall-E's girlfriend. Or just his friend that's a girl. But fuck, I'm only human. I sputter. I prove it once again. For your eyes, and your eyes only.

My uncle is going to send one of his friends to install a chandelier in my hospital room. I'm going to arrive in a limousine. In the meantime, I welcome you to my exhibition. I have a black heart-shaped shoulder bag. I open it, find pages inside. I tell you to pick one, like they're fortune cookies. The message reads: *You're beautiful when you cry.*

Religious feelings,
The smoke turns white,
The bag stays black.

Anna Ketamine

In a small white room, hanging on the back wall.

Jesus, crucified on a spiderweb of black tubing.

The coagulated blood on his extremities is made of rubies.

Warning. Any resemblance to real persons is intentional. Every cliché evoked has actually been lived. You are condemned to remember in this book. You can always put it down. It's not too late. It's never too late to put down a book. Or to fold the newspaper back up and turn off the TV. Or to stop eating. Or to shut everyone out. Or to cling to the past. Your hands. You decide. You're the hero.

Warning. If I'm forced to change your name, I'm going to shit all over your entire childhood, call you Stanislas instead of Samuel, and shit all over your entire childhood. Make you pick it all up every night with a shovel, and nobody to hold the bag.

Warning. If you're in my life, there's a chance you'll find yourself in my book. If I pass you on the street, there's a chance you'll find yourself in my book. I take photos of everything; I write poems. If I find your outfit disappointing, I'll put you in something purple. So that you match the book, at least. If I find your job disappointing, I'll find you a better one. If I find your life disappointing, I'll invent another one for you, a more exciting one. What's actually truly interesting are the moments of solitude. Since I'm not there when you're alone, I'll have to imagine them.

ANNA KETAMINE

I was wearing a purple dress. It was the day of my opening. I was a little surprised it was going so well. All I did was paint clouds on big neon skulls. Chill out. All the media attention was because of my friend. Victoria Love. She has brain cancer, a cloud tumour. I dedicated these pieces to her. The newspapers called. She told them everything. She always tells everyone everything.

I wear my best clothes when I go to see her. Accessories, a belt. I tell my clothes: behave, you might end up in a novel. A Québécois novel. Nobody reads in Quebec. No time to mess around. That must be why Victoria Love turned to experimental film. The least lucrative career choices ever.

I listen to music on my big beige sectional couch. Everyone wants a sectional couch this year. There are none left on Kijiji that look any good. Black Friday, black every other day. Pierre Dorion was at the Musée d'art contemporain. Walking through his exhibition was like walking through Kijiji. For ten bucks. Photos of bedrooms, photos of a lot of empty rooms. Paintings, sorry. Paintings that look like photos.

What I do at my job is a bit like Pierre Dorion's work. My new job. Thanks, Victoria Love. She put in a good word for me. She knows people everywhere. Now more than before. I find adjectives to summarize. I do the classifieds. I turn photos into adjectives. I know Kijiji. I spend a lot of time on it at work. It's like a reference book.

I used to be a museum guide. I had to explain the artworks and artists to visitors. Children in particular. I hate children. I hate anything that shrieks. Easy girls on Saint Laurent and children. I avoid Saint Laurent at night. I'm no martini girl, I don't wear G-strings. I stay home in my little one-bedroom apartment in Pointe-Saint-Charles and do my homework.

I have nine lives, like a cat. Lucky for me. I need them. When I play *Super Mario*, I can never find my guy. They got it right with the design of the WII controller. It vibrates when you die. It vibrates constantly. I think I do it on purpose, unconsciously. To get used to the idea of my death, maybe. At the book fair in Rimouski, a woman picked up Victoria Love's book to read the back. And then she put it down again, avoiding looking at her. It's heavy, cancer and death and all that. I wish books were more interactive. Like the controller. That books would vibrate at the end of each chapter. There would be no more than eight. But that's not how life works. What is death like? Do you vibrate? Do the words GAME OVER appear? Or is it the whole thing with the white light and the tunnel?

Before, she was Lili, Erection Assistant. She was a lot of things. This book could be called *Your Tarantino Dialogues* or *Special Requests*. She talks about film all the time. She never stopped saying that she was going to write ten books and that she was going to live ten more years. That it would be called *Experimental Film*. *Drama Queens* is like the book's stripper name.

I'm the same Anna, the one in Victoria Love's first book. Now I am Anna, Classified Ads Assistant, I work on the same floor as Victoria Love. We share a coffee card. We share everything. She's an amazing friend. We go to galleries together. Sometimes we bitch a little. I go into the first room of the exhibit. There's a big pink skull on the floor. I wonder whose skull it is. It's covered in symbols. What's that smell? Like chai. Or good quality incense. Pink is usually not her colour. But she wanted to be a pony. Drama queen. We're unicorns. I hold a highlighter to my forehead. I'm a unicorn. Hold a phallic shape to your head. A pencil. A dildo. It's magic, you're a unicorn too. Like her mother in her first book. Like me, Anna Ketamine, right now. You don't have to read all her books. You don't have to have read the first one to understand the second, but it's better. There will be ten in all. That's a lot. The highlighter is blue.

Blue of Highlighter. A book by Georges Bataille. The obsession with sensation. Sensationalism. A constant. Cheesy sentences, and now adjectives that more or less describe. That describe not well but enough. Only ever dipping one toe in.

We run into Maggie Books at the building's lost and found. I don't think anybody comes here to lose things. She's looking through the hats. Victoria Love draws a cloud on the one she picks. With a salamander in the corner.

"If my legs are like Jell-O and I can't get into bed, I'll slither. In the morning, I'm not a unicorn. I'm a reptile. I slither around the whole apartment."

While she slithers, I'm in my little apartment in Pointe-

Saint-Charles being a unicorn. Maggie slips a piece of paper into my jacket.

Zombie Scripters
A TARANTINO FILM
Getting a beer from the fridge witha walker
is not easy. But that won't stop our hero,
Michael Jackson, the bandit. Yes, the same leader
of the pack who buried an old couple alive
with his compatriots, who forced them to reveal
their banking information. Michael Jackson, the
badass mother-burier, didn't have an easy time
in prison. They left him his two legs, but not much
else. Hence the walker. What luxury.
Close-up of his hand: a can of PBR in a Ziploc bag.
Trailer-park style. Through the window, a bunch of
zombies, a bunch of green students with paper and
pencils. Michael opens his beer, super chill, and
sits on his couch,lifting his walker in the air and
waiting for them. One scratches at the door.
"Come here with your pencil so I can
make myself a straw."
THE END

Britney Speaks

The idea: a person giving themselves a pep talk in the mirror. "I am beautiful, I am smart, the world is mine."

The body of Britney Spears with a round mirror encircling her face. Next to her, a giant mirror someone's marked up with lipstick. In place of "Britney," there are motivational statements, cool self-affirmations. "Hot mamacita SPEAKS." "Girl next door SPEAKS." "Suck my pussy SPEAKS."

_____ SPEAKS
_____ SPEAKS
_____ SPEAKS
  BRITNEY SPEARS

The SPEAKS are all written in gemstones and the P, E, A, and R of the last one in miniature pears.

It smells so good in the apartment. I'm making white chocolate and orange cookies. I need to eat when I'm down. I've gone to a lot of restaurants alone in my life. In *The Waves*, Virginia Woolf describes a table. There are pear peels. I'm obsessed with this image. I'd like to eat those peels. For it to be like magic. I could retune literature with my life. I often make cookies or desserts with pears. That way I can say I accomplished at least one thing in my day. Either I made a batch of cookies or I wrote a good page. I can go to sleep smiling.

I was in the Miss Teen Québec pageant when I was younger. They came over, they saw I was cute, and it went from there. They took my money and, boom, spotlights. The process was simple. We did a series of activities. We were graded on our conversation, our level of participation, our bikinis, that kind of thing. The full range of our personalities, right? On the bus to the Beach Club, a girl told me she called her stupid friend her parakeet.

A few years later, Candy asked me what I was going to teach the world from the perspective of my nineteen years. I had no simple answer to her question. I was nineteen. I thought that was enough. Mathematics. Numbers are so important for people. If you're nineteen years old, you're automatically a little idiot. You're a new wine. Your life experiences smell like cork. Everyone knows that new wine sucks. It often comes from Australia. I have no desire to go to Australia. Part of travelling is tasting the wine of the region. I'll never see a kangaroo. I bought some for my fondue the other day. It tasted like chicken. Rabbit does too. Animals that hop taste like chicken.

Watching whatever random show comes on Canal D is a major activity for dancers who work at bars out in the sticks. These girls train themselves to enjoy doing the same things over and over. Full days identical to other days. Canal D, money, clients, frozen dinners, sleep.

Maude was on *Le Cercle* once, that game show Charles Lafortune used to host, one among many. My mother had bought me the board game. It was serious business. Maude was the first person I knew to be on television. I was proud to know her because of her bright pink hair. I saw Arnaud at my launch. He told me he'd been on the Quebec version of *Match Game*, another game show, this one hosted by Alexandre Barrette. He didn't win a cent. Neither did Maude, but at least they were on TV. Arnaud doesn't have pink hair, but I'm no less proud.

It's happened twice that I was watching *Come Dine with Me* with Britney and she's known one of the contestants because they'd worked together. Buffering. (The Internet sucks in hotels outside the city.) I also remember getting an email from Mathieu in Fermont. Click the link. The other dude from Incontinental, a band we really like, was the host for that episode. I think he made scallops. Or duck. Everyone always makes duck and rabbit on that show. The Québécois have a really lame idea of fine dining. I'm still traumatized by that tortoise soup.

We all have one stupid friend. God knows I've had a few. I find it amusing. Seasonal friendships. Girls to party with. Girly girls. Some of them more tomboyish. I tried the whole spectrum. Stupid girls are always better than TV. I can't snap my fingers, I can't whistle, I'm useless, but I smile like an idiot and I love them.

My favourite stupid friend is Britney. She's my little sweetheart. When her grandfather died, I took her to Parc Laurier with a blanket, a Scrabble set, and some old carrots so we'd have enough of a "picnic" to drink our six-pack of Boréale Blonde. I got forty-four points on *kiwi* and won. We have some great board-game stories. One time we were playing Cranium and she mimed *rising star*. She'd read the wrong side of the card.

I'm already looking forward to getting up tomorrow morning to eat a bowl of sugar cereal. The sun sets early. I open the fridge and think about tomorrow morning. We have milk, I'm all set. I can go to bed. Daydream about tomorrow, all alone in my big empty bed. Daydream about all that cereal. A stomach with whole-wheat polka dots. Healthy foods dance around me. Britney is going to be happy I'm thinking about wheat. She likes it when I eat asparagus, when I pamper my digestive system. When I talk to her about fibre, she rejoices. When I talk to her about royal jelly, she makes goat noises to make me laugh. I'm rewarded when I'm good to myself.

Yesterday I smoked a joint with Britney, a tiny one. It was a really bad idea. I felt uneasy in my body. I could feel my liver more than usual. I am a high Care Bear. An overmedicated Care Bear. On shuffle. Nobody knows anymore what does what, or why.

I'd like to grow old. Like, sixty-five plus. To be like the old lady in *Requiem for a Dream* and sit in my robe in front of the TV taking amphetamines. But I know I'd regret it, it would be like with the joint I smoked with Britney. It would seem like a good idea, an interesting experience, on paper, but in reality it would be the worst idea, the worst experience. Provocation is a bit like that. It's always prettier on paper. That's why we like literature. It is pretty and orderly on paper. Order is good. Origami is just as complicated as literature. You find a tutorial on YouTube, you follow every step perfectly. You're supposed to end up with a bird, you get a flower. OK. Too bad. Flowers are more poetic than birds. They're feminine, like pussy. Britney is at school at the Botanical Gardens. Today she dissected an orchid. I was writing. Everyone with their delicate little gestures for the universe. We tell each other about our days. She comes to see me every day. Britney Speaks in my ear. In fine print. She whispers lullabies to me. She puts my face in her boobs. Her breasts are aquatic. I can hear the sea, clearly. It's therapeutic. Drama queen in a plunging neckline. I'm with Britney. We begin our overview of the day.

"I got a massage from Hugues. Hugues had a thousand

dolphins. Little figurines, paintings, a dolphin pin on his business card. A thousand fennec foxes, a thousand dolphins. Everyone with their obsession."

"I had to count cocks. It makes me laugh every time I think about it. One cock, two cocks."

"A thousand cocks."

"Mathieu told me about a line from a film, something that exploded into 'a thousand shits.'"

"Mathieu has good taste in movies. A thousand is a good number for everything."

"Much better than ten."

"Yesterday, I watched *Life of Pi* with my mother. The tiger was making himself a little zebra bourguignon. At one point, they end up on an island. There are prairie dogs everywhere. The tiger's making himself a snack. He feels like he's got everything and a bag of chips. That's my mother's saying. She says that taking care of me gives meaning to her life. Pi writes the same thing about the tiger. I don't know what to say. Maternal love is so beautiful. I hope I have that in me."

Britney comes over to distract me after her classes. We don't do anything special. Chain-smoke, watch TV. She listens to me vent about stupid stuff. I put on a show.

"The family hour, all the game shows, *Come Dine with Me*, the Stella Artois ad with the Christmas greyhounds. Is there anyone left in Quebec who hasn't been on TV? Animal or human. Anyone?"

"I raise my glass to your shining armour and to this wonderful night with you."

We talk about sex. Girls love talking about sex. Britney

28

makes us tea in fancy little cups with flowers and saucers. I'm totally naked, I'm a mess of stretch marks at the table, but the flowers and the saucer excuse everything. I'm still putting on my show. Britney has to stop herself from photographing everything. My dildo lying fallow in the dresser drawer at the end of the bed. It needs to be within reach, a bicep curl away. No complicated origami. Napkin body. Crotch at the centrefold. Can't have to get up. Can't walk.

"If my vagina is a magazine, which lip is the cover?"

"That depends where you start reading."

"That means that, technically, on one side, the cover is my clitoris and the other is my anus?"

"It means that, in your vagina, you have an editor, his secretary, the columnists, an accountant, telephones with a bunch of lines, a peanut machine, a webmaster, an IT guy, trombones, a cleaning lady, a security guard, printers."

"Yes, I have laser-jet discharge."

Maggie made up a little film scenario to entertain us later. Britney reads it to us at the table as we sip our tea:

Texas Chain-Smoke Massacre
A FILM BY HARMONY KORINE
Britney Speaks and Victoria Love
are at a dimly lit table. The game's down to them.
Everyone went all in too quickly. Like mafiosos.
Ryan Gosling deals. The smoke stinks up the
basement. There is a concerto of suspicious sounds
upstairs. Metal clinking, mostly. Josée Yvon shows up,
panicked, with a tutu. Apparently some freak just
sawed off Marie Uguay's leg with his chainsaw.

Chloe Sevigny follows with feathers in her ass and a fresh pack of bitch sticks. Dakota Fanning is too drunk. She's taking pictures of her pussy in the mirror with a phone that was lying on the table. The sounds upstairs grow louder. The dealer announces a flush. Everyone falls into Sevigny's pack. Even Ryan. Bitch sticks are not very masculine. It sounds like someone upstairs is washing sharp knives in a metal sink.

THE END

Maggie Books

The room you enter is irritating. Too much noise, too many people in uniform. Don't worry. They're all actors. Keep your bag in your pocket. A USB key is a police siren. It is inserted in the doorknob of a front door. The door is covered in blood. To show that the investigation is still open on a bloody murder.

A film critic who makes lists of films
    she'd like to see.
To amuse herself.
But she doesn't show them to anyone.

Or a graphic designer who works for a newspaper.
Her name is Maggie.
She sees everything.
The advice columns.
The big investigative stories.
The classifieds.
The "I saw you did you see me" ads.

Screenplays to react to the way the newspaper treats her.
Screenplays to react to the news she lays out on the page.

MAGGIE BOOKS

The descriptions of films are tiny chandeliers. I prefer little things to big ones. Sometimes I centre everything on the page for fun. I shrink the margins and the page is filled right away. A little chandelier, an uvula of words. It makes me smile like Dakota Fanning. Sometimes I have to wait a long time for new documents. I sit in my office, I wait for someone to send me the pixilated logo and the bad photo, I wait my turn. I warm up my graphic tablet, I play with its clitoris with my fairy hands. Graphic design is a real girl-on-girl activity. You stroke and pet things that are a little cold. Very precise, detail-oriented work.

I'm a current-events girl. Even my stomach is up to date. Right now and as of a few months ago, I'm allergic to gluten. It's very complicated. I have to seem all fancy ordering carafes of red wine. I ask for the menu, I choose a wine. It was different before. I'd arrive at the bar, order a pint. I'd never specify which kind. I'd tip a dollar and down the first drink in one shot. God, the thirst when you've spent the whole day waiting. I don't dare go to the same places anymore. First, the wine sucks there, and second, getting drunk on wine is expensive. Either I drink it by the glass (and the glasses are very small) or I look like a big alcoholic walking around my friends' table with a pitcher of sangria. With my straw and my orange-slice smile. Yes, I can eat oranges. Maggie, can you eat rice? Maggie, can you eat bread? Inviting me for dinner is complicated. Oh universe, how many text messages have been sent from grocery stores around the world because of we who are allergic to gluten? Oh universe, gluten, what the fuck?

The shower door suddenly opens behind me. I arch my back, my wet hair tickling my upper back in slow motion.

A hand on my hip, I make eyes at the shameless voyeur interrupting me in the shower. There's nobody there. I put on my little skank show for an empty bathroom. The mirror laughs at me a little. I didn't get myself a sweet romantic, no. I got myself a guy with a cheap shower with a door that opens by itself. I won't be taking any more taxis to Hochelaga-Maisonneuve. Too many old buildings, too many chances of ending up in showers with doors that open by themselves. Something hot slides down my right leg. We didn't use protection. Resolutions for 2013: no more HoMa, but more latex. I'm getting too old for magical thinking. Silver screen, shower scene.

"Maggie, can you, like, put the photo in the centre with my article on either side? It'd be funny to see Mahée Paiement, like, in her fancy gown, saying that breastfeeding is glamorous with a brooch on her pussy. Like, a big sequin on a pile of shit."

Start by considering words other than *like*, whatever your name is. Everyone is whatever-your-name-is here. We fool around. Crack each other up. But we have no illusions: everything is fake, latex, plastic, even your crown. We work for an image industry. One image, one second, and we move on to the next. One among many others. Everyone has the right to their two little minutes of glory, but it doesn't last long. I'm a number in the telephone of the guy I slept with yesterday. I live in an eternal morning after. A girl I went to high school with wrote me to say that she wants to become a journalist. She had this epiphany while watching a lake freeze over or something like that. I imagine she was telling me this because it says on my Facebook that I work at *La*

Presse. I wrote back saying she should start by putting capital letters at the beginning of her sentences. Not everyone has a sense of humour.

I watched a documentary on Marie Uguay recently.
She said she felt like a grain of sand.
Me too.
You too.
I am jealous of all these people for whom life is like an
    all-inclusive at Playa del Carmen.
Who's Carmen?
I want a beach too.
Playa del Marie-Soleil Tougas.
Playa del Ève Cournoyer.
Playa del Michael Jackson.

I wonder if Renée Martel and Lise Watier read Asimov when they were young.

I wonder if Marie Uguay was treated like a slut the way I am.

"Maggie, could you make it so the ad for the new Lady Gaga perfume falls on the page opposite my article about rashes that look like the Virgin Mary?"

Journalists are pretty funny. I can't complain. They're not all serious like you'd imagine. They make me wait, sure. Sometimes for a long time. Almost everything is last minute. I have to rush around in Photoshop, do overtime I won't get paid for. I spend my whole day waiting. Everyone knows I love spending my time on silly projects. Nothing serious leaves my office in internal mail before five or six o'clock.

I get ridiculous requests all day long. I have great abs but also a very good digestive system. It's a pain in the ass to play the clown for everyone. Charles told me I should write stand-up. I have only two subjects. Death and stupid girls. I'd like to have an effect on even one person, or a few. One to start. I'd like to have a job that's a little more artistic. I'm not asking for much. I just want to do more than basic layouts. Layouts ordered by someone. We're doing a special section for the holidays. The page numbers will be red. They asked me to come up with a little icon to go around the page numbers. I face a pressing choice between a snowman, a reindeer, a mistletoe, or Santa. That's it, the artistic part of my job. Choosing the non-perishable item for the food drive. Choosing the hand for the handcuffs. Choosing the photo that will best enhance the retrospective of the life of Renée Martel. She's not from my generation. Apparently she has cancer. Everyone has cancer. Everything gives you cancer. I'm pretty lucky with my gluten. It's the soft porn of health problems. Britney's grandmother's heart is on the right side instead of the left. She has to take about forty pills a day. They told her she'd live to thirty, at best, and she's now seventy. Britney's friend is a writer. She was on *Tout le monde en parle*. I saw her huge face framed in feathers on my way home from work a few months ago. But in her case, it's inoperable. She's going to die from her brain cancer. Either that or in a car accident. The other night, Britney told me her friend had decided she was going live for ten years and write ten books. I find that charming. Positive thinking. I just write screenplays:

Gogo Mango
Series adapted from the graphic novel
EPISODE FIVE
"Stroboscopic Society"
The taxis are yellow New York cabs.
They explode on the pavement. Like popcorn.
The street is the esophagus. It implodes.
Geysers of butter erupt from sewers.
Gogo Mango emerges from a wave of trans fat,
surfing on a book. Little 8-bit conqueror theme song.
She's on cortisone. When the cortisone is gone,
her superpowers fade. It's the episode where
she traces her scars with a golden pencil.

THE END

It was Charles who showed me how to draw. Each panel has to get right to the point. I should say that Charles gave me only one lesson. Those hands that showed me how to draw the contours of a character had already slid down the contours of my own body. My beautiful goddess hips, the curves of my soul. I thanked him. This process of detachment from my body is long and arduous. I'm haunted by a thousand sensorial flashbacks when I'm in the presence of an old flame. The problem is that all my friends are guys I have a history with. Guys that have seen me naked.

I have to google Renée Martel to choose a picture. She has beautiful, shiny blond hair. Her old photos remind me of Lise Watier at the height of her youth. I saw her on *Les enfants de la télé* when I was flipping through the channels a few weeks ago. In the Plateau, we watch TV by flipping channels. We don't advertise the fact that we're Vidéotron clients. We talk openly about the new annual membership we got for peanuts at Boîte Noire. Everyone needs to know about this deal. Before asking your geek friend to show you how to download movies, drop by the Boîte Noire and spend a quick half-hour. You will no longer want to know anything about the outside world. You'll go home with your purse full of rectangular cases, your wallet proudly carrying your new membership card; you'll cancel on your geek friend and proudly turn on this television, this DVD player, and watch them make out. You have a penis and don't carry a purse? They have little plastic bags just for you. In the meantime, I have to choose a photo of this lady. Overtime has begun. I'm a natural blonde. I suspect both Lise and Renée of cheating.

Sweet Home Dollarama
A MICHAEL SNOW FILM
A blond girl sleeps on a pullout couch
beneath a second-floor window. The last four letters
of "Dollarama" are in the shot, quivering slightly.
The camera doesn't move for twenty minutes.
THE END

I live above the Dollarama at Mont-Royal and Papineau. My roommate was the one who signed us up for Vidéotron. Nobody knows we have it as long as the TV is off. He was also the one who insisted we share groceries, which suits me fine, given my schedule. I bought him an apron for Christmas. He always makes dinner. His name is Benjamin and he's a year and a few months older than me. There are a few bars on my route home from work. When I finish late, I hang around L'Esco till last call. I always find a few friends for the night. The barmaid must think I'm easy. I don't care. She doesn't know anything about my life. I met Benjamin there, at L'Esco. We've never slept together but I know he has a big cock. I can't count the number of times he's ended the night with his cock out, making everyone uncomfortable. It doesn't make me uncomfortable at all, cocks just make me laugh. I understand visceral sex more than romance. I'm always embarrassed when the lovers kiss for the first time in movies. When I was little, I'd go so far as to cover my eyes. But lay your dick on the table and I'll barely react. Benjamin's is big, I kind of want to use it but I don't want to endanger our friendship. Things always become fragile when you start mixing relationships. I'm the kind of girl who cooks dishes with just one spice. If I put in turmeric, I won't add curry. I make decisions.

Writing books.
Like you smoke cigarettes.
Like you eat pasta with butter.
Books.
That's it, a writer's work.
How are those cigarettes?
What's in this pasta?

The hands of the one who consumes and prepares,
    they're yours.
We know.
You're always talking about yourself.

And these shoulders. Have you seen these magnificent shoulders? One shoulder, and another identical shoulder on the other side. But in reverse. A right shoulder and a left shoulder. Symmetrical. Two shoulders. Have you seen the shoulders on this little bit of a woman?

Poor-girl shoulders. Little links, bones, a bit of meat, almost enough. You won't make a big book with that. Almost too little.

I took the decorations off the Christmas tree while Benjamin was at work. I replaced them with Valentine's Day decorations. I kept the big star for the top. My birthday is the day after Valentine's. It's my birthday tree too! I made almost all the decorations myself, with red construction paper. There are a lot of little paper teardrops all over the floor. Little asses and cleavages. That's what happens when you cut out hearts. Benjamin's poor little heart when he finds out that I've been cheating on him, that I have other men in my life. I'm the only one who can tell him. Or plan to tell him. There's never a good moment. Drama queen.

My fortune cookie tells me nothing about my night. There is a prospect of a thrilling time ahead of you. I'm going to fuck in a church tonight. That's the thrilling time. We already did it yesterday, but it's no less thrilling. Less spontaneous and exciting, sure. But come on, a church, that's like forty points in casual-sex bingo. There's no little asterisk specifying that it has to be for the first time. I think you even get more points for repeat visits. You know, nobody imagines it's the kind of activity you can repeat.

I look at the big photo of Victoria Love and I think about

her. I think about all those years of bad luck promised by broken mirrors. Someone else took care of breaking them for her. Everyone knew someone who had cancer before her. Everyone reminds her of it. You don't feel any less like crying because of the plurality. Someone who beat it, someone who died of it, the stories don't put recovery at the top of the agenda. What's important is that while you tell the story (for whom? why?), you say that you understand. God, how everyone understands. Everyone empathizes. It's crazy how predictable it is. I'd like it if someone were to be happy that it was happening to me. I have a friend who has cancer. I'd like it if someone wished me even more pain. I can take more. A little headache here or there isn't going to dim our smiles.

As I was saying, fucking in a church. God doesn't go there anymore. It's a space now, a rehearsal space for Rémi and his friend. They do circus stuff, they need space to throw around their hoops. The woman from the organization has no idea what they're up to. She's not wondering if one of her tenants is fucking a girl in the confessional and right out in the middle of all the pews.

I'd rather not get my ass soaking wet
    when I sit.
I sat on a bench in Parc Baldwin in front of the church.
I have an anglophone ass. I prefer to fuck and come
    in English.
Shoot the shit. The shit hits the fan.

I feel like an inspired college student. I want to stop people in the street and ask them existential questions. Everyone has already witnessed this kind of scene, or been interrupted themselves by this kind of person. At the entrance to the metro, for example. While you're waiting to meet someone at the top of the escalators at the Mont-Royal metro. While you're wondering if the other person is possibly waiting to meet you at the bottom of the escalators. You ask yourself if the specified meeting place was just in your head, and then here is a young man interrupting the flow of your thoughts. I feel like that guy, the half hobo, half middle-class kid, his forehead slick with sweat, disturbing the peace of the people around him, trying to destabilize the order of things with two questions. Look at how stupid this is! Look at how badly this was done! I haven't only just realized this, unlike the college kid. You see me on my park bench with my wine-coloured trench coat and you think: *That girl is no student, that girl is in business.* That girl has short blond hair, a concave mushroom cut that's a little bit off, just a little. Her haircut is almost level, only crooked enough to inspire doubt. That girl is wearing a sweater and black leggings, the same clothes as yesterday. That girl slept on a clothesline, as my mother would say.

I wonder what Benjamin will have made for dinner. I feel like texting him to ask but it's better if I keep my phone in my desk drawer when I'm working overtime. Otherwise I'll never get out of here. I'm so hungry. I see smoked meat sandwiches floating over the smooth blond face of Renée Martel. I want to make a montage and send it to Benjamin. It's tough to just turn serious on a dime. I dreamed I was eating butter chicken last night. My hair is the same colour as the sauce. Maybe everything is connected. Maybe I drank too much coffee. Maybe Renée doesn't give a shit that we're talking about her in our little holiday section. She definitely doesn't. She's busy having cancer. When you've got that, you have to forget about it. Which is what she seems to be doing. It says in the article that she's on tour. I'll go with Benjamin. That's how I pay him back. With free tickets. And box wine. He helps himself to my supply. It doesn't bother me a bit. No waste, no time to fool around. My phone vibrates in the drawer. The accounts have arrived. If time is money, gluten is a hundred-dollar bill, blood in the stool. There's a hole in my bucket, Dear Liza, and the grocery bill never stops draining my bank account. Good thing Benjamin pays the Vidéotron bill. My life is expensive lately.

Renée Martel in a bikini on a tropical beach
    with feathers in her ass.
The water is golden.
Like the sauce of my butter chicken.
Fuck it, I'm ordering food.
The smell won't bother anyone.
I'm all alone here.

Darth Horse
A little girl is drinking a giant
chocolate milkshake in a booth at an
American truck stop. Jean-François Harrison
sits down across from her. The little girl is blond,
she looks like Dakota Fanning. Super close-up
of her lips sucking away on the straw. A little smile.
Jean-François subtly slips her a wad of bills. Brown
bills. But American money is all the same colour.
Black-and-white economy. Like magic. Next shot:
the little blond girl is at the racetrack with her father.
He's excited, she's cool, still with her little smile.
A horse wins. The father leaps toward his daughter.
Cut. Back to the truck stop. Katie Holmes sets down
a big vanilla milkshake and a coffee. The little girl
takes big gulps without the straw. Her father hands
her some bills. She runs to throw up in the
bathroom. She drank too much sugar too quickly

for one day. She looks up as she comes back out.
Guy Turcotte is pinning up a poster
for Dakota Fanning's next film: *Darth Horse.*

THE END

Bettie Sage

You are among a group of spectators who enter a dark room. An enormous Tylenol tablet appears on the ceiling. You hear a recording of the Tylenol speaking in a maternal, comforting voice. A bit like in relaxation recordings: "You are calm, you feel light." A trap door opens and little Tylenol tablets tied to fishing line fall from the ceiling like rain. Again, it's like in a relaxation recording, when it tells you to listen to the rain falling on your tent.

At the end, the Tylenol turns green, as if to say the exercise is over and you can continue on your way. You leave the room. You have all just done E together.

The sun is shining every day. Every day I get up early, I see the sun, sometimes big, often small. Shining like a good sun. I'm like the sun too. I shine every day. I do simple things, a lot of big important writing one day, a lot of little nothings the next. Are we playing? Let's play. Let's play at answering the question that kills. What will we not be doing tonight? A lot of things. So many things. We will not be going to see the Keith Kouna show. We will not be doing coke off the bruised breasts of a prostitute. We will not be going out for beers with friends. We will not be taking the metro. We will not be trying to lock eyes with anyone in the frenzied crowd. There will be no little moments of collusion. We will not be throwing our panties at the singer because it would take too long to get them off. I'd fall down. We will not be following the singer through the streets. We can't even run. There are no big goons at the entrance to check the list for your name, but if there was one, he'd say: Who are you, little mango-faced girl, to ask to see the artist? Who are you? What are you? I want to take my clothes off for the artist, sir. I want him to see me naked. I can do that, take my clothes off. It takes longer, the movements are less fluid than before, but I can do it. I'm really good at it. The sun is shining every day on my mottled skin. I have stretch marks. I look like I caught Wolverine in the bathroom. Raw. On TV, they recommend emu oil. Apparently it gets rid of them. You wake up one morning and you have big marks on your hips. You think about Freddy. It must be Freddy's fault. I could tell my mother. Maman, Maman, I was totally naked like a big girl. I showed him everything. He said nothing. It felt good. My mother has to measure all my body parts. They want my measurements for an interview. Neck, arms, hips. My hips. With my stretch marks. Notches on my belt. They're going to take my photo, they're going to dress me in pretty clothes. The stylist is going to find me pretty clothes like she found for Léo Bureau-Blouin. I am going to have the same stylist as Léo Bureau-Blouin. The sun is shining every day on my head and the head of Léo Bureau-Blouin too. Everyone is talking about it. Everyone will be talking about it for a long time. About the little girl who put out a book. But mostly about her cancer. Poor little girl with the tumour in her head. That cloud tumour. Oh, how poetic. A cloud, like that, in her head. Oh, that big pussy. That slack, torn-up pussy. Tiger pussy. Wolverine and Freddy. Team-work. The sun is shining every day and every day I take pills. The sun shines on my pills but not brightly enough this morning because I nearly mixed up my night pills with my morning pills. I'm not sure I answered the questionnaire they sent me well enough. I fell asleep between two silly

49

questions about the contents of my Kindle. I should finish writing my answers before I forget. The drama queen, the great woman of letters, doesn't feel like any less of an idiot in her document. You can't say that in the questionnaire. You can't say that on TV. TV is for talking about emu oil, not literature. The sun is shining every day, so thank the sun for living on. Accept every invitation. I have my orange purse because today I'm taking the orange line. I'm going to Bonaventure metro for the book fair. I take the metro. I'm no big star. I don't arrive in a limo. I'm just metropolitan. That's something at least. You should see me on a bike. It doesn't work. I don't know how to stay upright. I break down everywhere. I'm a dead leaf. Take the metro all alone. Get impossibly stressed doing simple things. It doesn't cost much to get stoned. Two birds with one stone. What is the measurement of your neck, little girl? Let's take your photo. Then we'll talk. We're going to chat. Just gab. This sun that shines every day. Every day full of the promise of a better book. Another book. The next one? What's it going to be like? What'll it be about? Who will it be about? There's nobody left. You've eaten everyone, and what's more, you're not even dead. Put on your pretty clothes. Put on that expensive little scarf. Leave your house. All lit up. Go meet the ladies and the gentlemen. Write something, everyone's looking at you. Say something cute, everyone's listening. Being a writer is exhausting. You write down everything you think. You mustn't say it. There's no point in raising your voice. There's not much point in seeing people. Socializing, society, all that: it's for idiots. Entertainment: not for me. I make them myself, my films and my shows. My desires, my obsessions. The usual backdrop: absent father, all-controlling mother. Mother making faces as she passes her daughter at the computer. Maman, you're interrupting my writing, you're distracting me. Maman, you're blocking half the screen. Half is already too much. I didn't like *Film Socialisme*. I wasn't made for dictatorship. I'm not so sweet and nice for all that. Anyway, you're the one who dies first in the horror movie. I don't know you. You're the girl I slept with one drunken night. The girl I promised a role. I'm a producer from LA. My breath smelled like McDonalds when I was waking up this morning, and your number was written on my arm. Maman, Maman, come save me. I'm surrounded. I don't know any magic tricks but I pretend. I shuffle the cards, I ask you to choose one. And then I abandon the whole thing. You find this incredible. The sun is shining every freaking day, and this too is incredible.

Paradise: Golf

Guns, black children, more guns, revolution,
Rebelle, the Quebec film. Female directors suck.
Except Sofia Coppola. Sofia plays eighteen holes
against Kim Thúy. Kim wins, she always wins.
In a dress. Every piece of clothing in the world
would be more beautiful on Kate Winslet. Her
father doesn't have to tell her. The golf balls
came with a bottle of Grey Goose. Might
as well find a use for them.

THE END

Christine Mango

You enter another room. The gallery is huge. A man is fucking a goat on a Twister mat. His hands and feet, and the goat's paws too, placed on all the circles of the game.

Dollar signs in the goat's eyes.

A glowing sign reads BINGO in flashing bulbs.

Tons of coins and American dollar bills fall from the sky. A bit like balloons on New Year's Day.

I collapse on the ground. They should just put chairs out if they want to prevent that. The oncology clinic is for people who are really sick. Give me a chair, for fuck's sake. I'm orange. Like traffic cones, and tanning salon enthusiasts. They're going to show me in theatres and cinemas. Worst case, I die in this illusion. Nod yes. The actress who plays me is going to have a great time. It'll be a great challenge. She'll use a walker, type with one hand. She'll fall to the ground. Collapse. Demand a chair. The audience will want to get up. The first row of seats will empty out.

Give me a chair, for fuck's sake.

Give her a chair, for Christ's sake.

The actress will light a cigarette. Right in the middle of the oncology clinic. That sentence was difficult to write. I'm out of breath. Give me a chair, for fuck's sake. The pivot nurse brings her a wheelchair. Useless chair. I have to take off my boots. Fucking useless chair. They want to weigh me. I've gained fifty pounds. Jesus. Who do I sue? McDonalds? Cadbury? I wouldn't know where to begin. I'm a huge cow. A huge living cow, I tell myself. But I'm going to die. I hadn't thought of that. Dying and all that. Don't think about it.

They need to give me a platform to express myself.
Make relevant suggestions.
Put more chairs in your clinics.
Touch people.
Say something to them.
Nothing important.
She is going to write a great book.
For the moment, she's doing nothing.
She hangs from the bus pole.
Just above the people sitting.
Her liver hurts.
She can feel it in her torso.
It's not exactly that it hurts, but she can feel it.
It affects her appreciation of life.

I'm hanging from a pole because nobody gave me their seat. I didn't ask, I should say. The sign reserving the accessible seats near the front doesn't have a little picture of a twenty-three-year-old woman with a liver that wants to escape her body. There's a pregnant woman, an old person, an injured person, but no young woman with a crazy liver. It's hard to explain. It would take at least a paragraph. Paragraphs get in the way. I want to get off the bus to smoke a cigarette. I would like to sit down. On a park bench. Outside. To not be moving. The bus moves and purrs. The pussy razor purred too. It reminded me of the sounds from the MRI machine. A beautiful memory. That was right before the appointment, the magical appointment. The doctor had said that my head was fine, that I was going to live without disruptions or worries for three more months. Three months at a time. There could always be unpleasant surprises after that interval, but that's not something to think too much about. Like how I need to forget the liver that wants to escape. Life is full of disagreeable things for a sick person. You can't take offence. You have to take it all with a grain of salt. And buy some coarse salt for the grinder later at the grocery store. That'll be an activity for me. Britney used my mother's pussy razor to trim my hair. That's a beautiful memory too. The bus is a place that lends itself to memories.

I am the daughter of a bus driver and I'm afraid to take the metro. Daddy issues much? I'm the daughter of a metro ticket agent. His biological daughter and everything. I'm seriously afraid. Shaking. I play vibrator on the bench. Shake like a leaf in the wind. The poles on the bus are something familiar at least. That and my father, if he's there. Kisses everywhere. I'll never make love again. I've never made love with my father either. I've never put my father's penis in my mouth, I'm not Christine Angot. I've done a lot of things. I've put a lot of other penises in my mouth. I'll keep doing things. I'll even do things especially for and with you. Just for you, the hands. Yes, you and your mysterious future, reader. I say "mysterious" because you're also just a concept in the end. We don't know who you could be in a hundred years. We know only that you are going to have hands, and even that isn't necessarily true.

I listen to loud, raging music. Dada Life. "Happy Violence." I can't go see my favourite artists perform. I go to bed at the same time they get up. I envy musicians so much. Other people's bodies move beneath their fingers. I seem pretty boring with my words. I have little power over things. You need a lot of hair to dance to dubstep. I do it in thought. I have the obligatory short hair. That's how you can tell the cancer patients in the waiting room. During their shows, the dudes from Dada Life dump out a big bottle of champagne. I've seen pictures. There's always a goon walking around dressed up as a banana.

I have to learn how to be alive. I think nobody really knows how to do it right. Look at Michael Jackson. Look at Marie-Soleil Tougas. Look at the American as much as the Québécois. Dead people seem perfect precisely because they're dead. You never read things like: *"She was constantly picking her nose when she was little," said a close family friend of Marie-Soleil Tougas.* My new life can be sad. It still depends on sentences. With sentences you make paragraphs, and with paragraphs you make books. Books. The word looks up at me, insistently. What time is it? Already. It goes quickly. I didn't even have the time to say something interesting. It's already the next day. I have to take pills again. A handful of frozen blueberries, a handful of frozen strawberries, four spoonfuls of vanilla yogourt, five fresh raspberries, about a cup of milk. In the blender, and then in a tall glass with a blue straw. Look at Facebook, send an email to Mathieu, tweet a photo of my berry smoothie.

My morning pills.

Read in the bath, *Un verre de bière mon minou*, by Louis

Geoffroy. Feel like drinking, like putting down the book. Neither happens. I stay in the tub, piss in it, finish the book. I wonder who could possibly want to masturbate in my vagina. No answer. Don't look at myself in the mirror. The last pages of the book in the now-icy water.

My midday pills.

Shepherd's pie with merguez, prepared by me with love before my mother comes home from work. For dessert? *Un verre de milkshake mon minou.* I am going to wear this blender out. I'm a little afraid it will explode. That the blade will spin out of control, fly off, and slice open my esophagus. Cause of death: blender accident. This kind of paranoia is why I shouldn't smoke pot.

My dinnertime pills.

Patrick Straram tells me what he's reading. I feel bad imposing my reading list on you. I read all his books. You don't have to. I can sum them up. His books are hard to find. The whole counterculture section in general. I was feeling revolutionary.

My nighttime pills.

I just got up in the middle of the night to eat some fruit. Fruit is so fucking good. I ate a pear on the couch. I always have to keep my back arched, but on the couch it's not too bad. I woke up with the TV on, Canal D blasting. I'd fallen asleep on the couch. I woke up worried. Michael Jackson appeared in my dream. He wasn't doing much. He was wearing sequined clothing and standing in the corner. Like a latent subject for the next dream. Just like on TV. Coming up next, soon, in thirty seconds.

Blue pill in case of insomnia.

I should find myself a pseudonym to make all this interesting. "She really inhabited the body of a sick girl. You can feel all the cortisone in her process. That acetaminophen breath, that syrupy voice. We suffocate along with her, follow her into her abyss." Don't do that, guys. Don't follow me into my abyss. It's not a good idea. Kisses everywhere. You touch your pants. You're embarrassed. You can't get an erection. It's normal. I'm not sexy anymore. I never understood why Britney found it so funny that I call even the grocery store clerks "my love." Now I understand. Nobody wants to be my love anymore. Nobody wants my kisses anymore. It's over. That's my abyss. I will descend into it all alone and shout back up to you about what I see there. Just what I see from below. You'll listen. We'll call it a testimony. They'll put it on TV. In the afternoon, while everyone's at work. You must work too. Do you ever get erections at work? I would be truly honoured if you used my book to hide your erection. Say if you had to walk by your colleagues. My first lover told me that erections happen randomly sometimes. His name was Julien. He had blond streaks in his hair and essential knowledge on the subject of erections. It had happened to him once before a presentation in class. He'd covered it up with a book. He only had a book. He looked crazy. Everyone looks crazy sometimes, but nobody really is. The truly crazy are too crazy to tell us about it. No testimonials, no TV. I slept all afternoon, because I'm overmedicated. My pills again. How many days have passed since the beginning of this book? I don't know anymore. Is it important? Is it relevant to talk about it? It would only really have an effect if I died in the interval. For the moment, I'm not dead. I am very much alive. I am a unicorn who kisses you everywhere. Kisses everywhere, monsieur. Kisses everywhere, madame.

Kisses Everywhere, that could be a title. That's how I used to sign off my texts to clients. My mouth: the only part of my body not affected by the cortisone. I'm retaining water. My cheeks are starting to become too heavy for my face. I don't know where to stop anymore when I put cream on my scars. I find myself a little ridiculous with my little jar. Trying to demarcate them. My face is not important. It's my fingers I have to polish. They're what's important. Their communication with my brain. I've always been obsessed with appearances. I can't help it. I'm a girl. The real deal. Drama queen. The skin of my face has the same texture as the skin of a mango. My face is a mango. Same texture. I compared them. I stroked a mango with one hand and my face with the other. I did that with my hands. My writer hands. In my dimly lit kitchen. Close your eyes and stroke a mango with your right hand and my face with your left, you won't feel a difference. I've done it, for real.

Poetry: hit Enter at the end of each line. To make life bearable. Me and Marie Uguay, we feel like grains of sand. I'm suspicious of myself because I'm ending my life with a period. When my life is supposed to be a poem. It's in my first book, google it.

I'm going to shoot myself in the foot writing this book. I don't care. I'm going to die. I'm going to write eight more books first. One per year, like François Blais. I'm not a snail like other writers. I'm here to bear witness, comfortably seated in my abyss. My feet up on the little footstool, surrounded by piles of paper.

60

Chlamydia Sinesis

You walk into a giant room. As big as the one that holds the permanent collection at the MAC. In front of you, a ton of mattresses lying side by side on the ground, like a huge square of soft sidewalk. Plain beige girls are frozen in the air, jumping from one mattress to the other, flowers covering their private parts. Beautiful in their innocence and light. You look up. On the ceiling, SLUTS is spelled out in diamonds, in what looks like Comic Sans.

I'm on the Internet. I'm using the wi-fi at the little tea shop. Tonight they are announcing the winner of the literary prize. I have the whole day before me. You call the server with a bell here. It makes me feel a bit too much like a princess for my liking. My mother gave me a little bell so I can call her in the apartment. We're in the Quartier Latin. A girl keeps walking back and forth in front of the window of the tea shop. She must be a prostitute. The customer at the table next to mine seems pretty disturbed by it. Our mothers all had a bit of a slutty phase. I like whores myself.

Michaela, a girl from high school, writes me on Facebook.

"What's new, Victoria Love? What have you been up to?"

"Lots of things. I'm a writer. I have brain cancer. For more information, google me."

Michaela has ended up as assistant manager at RONA. She's been with her boyfriend for a year. She's happy. I wonder what it feels like to be happy. I drink my coffee. I wait for my cereal to get soft. My pills wait for me to present them to my stomach. They're right there, on the counter, with my drinking yogourt. You can call the server with a bell in this place, they can definitely put up with me bringing my own creamy beverage. It's easier to swallow with a creamy drink. My taste buds were happy this morning. The raspberry yogourt is my favourite.

I left the tea shop. I went to meet Mathieu's couch. His Montreal couch. He moved to the city when he was young. Nature isn't for everyone. I take a nap so I'll be rested. Your face, like your intentions, is what counts for people. It's the first thing they see. Everyone is always asking me how I'm doing these days. I have a fat face. I look stupid all the time. I woke up with the word *papal* in my head. In my whole face. It's already time to get ready for the award ceremony.

My hairstylist is named Laurent. Yes, Laurent on Saint-Laurent. The receptionist didn't joke about it when I called. Hair is serious business for these people. I put on my makeup at a station belonging to a Lola. She isn't there.

My hairstylist asks me who cut my hair last. I don't dare tell him it was Britney with my mother's pussy razor. There are no other clients. I could say the word *pussy* without setting off the sprinklers. I could tell him I'm poor, I'm on welfare, but I'm a princess for the day. No, a queen. A queen doesn't have to show her bank statements to anyone. She puts on her crown and her sequins. I put more sparkles on my eyelids. Makeup is difficult. Especially when you don't know how to apply it. You have to put on several layers to get the results you want. Trying for a cat eye like in your fashion magazine? Mess up the proportions like I do, then hide it all with your blackened finger.

My head is a canvas, and Laurent is Riopelle. I would have liked a haircut more in the vein of Laurent Grasso. With neon and a ton of gel. A nineties cut. He's at the MAC right now and his name is Laurent too.

I moonwalked into the award ceremony. There was a huge photo of my face at the entrance. I felt like drawing horns on it. My face has changed so much since the photo was taken. I have such big cheeks. It's like heaven for pinching aunties.

The book that won the literary award tells the story of a guy. Once upon a time there was a guy. Fucking guys. His heart was replaced by a cauliflower. It's the story of a guy tripping on mushrooms. I have mushrooms in my mouth, it's a fungal situation, I could tell you all about it. But I still wouldn't have the cheque. Is that how money works? I lost part of a tooth eating cauliflower. Tell me that's how money works, that this isn't happening to me for nothing. I hadn't prepared a speech. It would have included the words *shit*, *fuck*, and *cunt*. In English, and not necessarily in that order. "Shit fuck cunt": a poem with three words and two holes. I'm not sure which of the three makes me lose the most money. I cry and I yell, "Shit fuck cunt." You like that, local gossips? Only stupid girls can publish books about stupid girls. Serial girlfriends. Disguise yourself a little. Try a pseudonym. Do something. But no. Huge photo. Get a blow-out for the launch. Write with fake nails, wait for copyright. But don't win, no. That's not how it works with money. I speak in English. I talk about cunts.

I could see myself on *Deal or No Deal*. Julie Snyder would say: "I've just received an offer. We'll give you the twenty-thousand-dollar prize for which you were nominated. But, in exchange, you'll have to accept a more messed-up body."

She places a small glass box before me. There's a big red EMERGENCY button underneath.

No deal. I can't handle it anymore, having the features of a sick person.

I'll ask my publisher to give me two thousand dollars for the copyright. I'll give presents to my mother and my friends. We'll drink blue drinks. We'll eat with our hands. It'll be ridiculous. It'll be messy. But that, at least, will last my whole life.

I would have said, "No deal," but before leaving I still took a minute to fill my purse with truffles. Pierre Karl Péladeau would have done the same thing, for sure. He would have had a purse ready. He seems like a man who appreciates sweets. Not that he's fat.

Back home, I asked my mother to shower me in all the stuffed animals she could find in the apartment. Yes, to shower me in them, I used that word. I'm a writer. A poet, maybe. My mother showered me in animals.

The next day, I have nothing to do when I get up. I decide to pick a few fights with people in comment threads. That's what blogs are for. I roam the Internet. Everyone wrote an article in 2013. Most of the action is happening on blogs. There's no editing process. Just a big blue button. I have a message. Samson reporting what my nemesis said. She speaks fucking bitch. I'd like to buy her a ticket to Cancun. Go on, girl. I cry with rage for the first time in my life. I can't see the screen anymore. I taste blood. I meow and I play the piano. I haven't been affected by words since Stanislas said that girls writing is like cats playing the piano. He was making a joke.

I am a stupid girl.
You are a stupid girl.
We are stupid girls.
Piss on us.
So we can be done with it.
Give us big cheques.
Give us suitcases.
You gotta spend money to make money.
An afternoon at Simons.

Bertrand Vergeture

On the wall in a small room: a baseball bat with neon-green troll hair, an abundance of spiders, neon-green car tracks, mouldy green waste that climbs, tracing the shape of a nose.

The face of Bertrand Vergeture.

My poet friends are coming for dinner. I'm making fondue bourguignonne. I used capital letters for all the sauces. I made three to go with our fondue. Peanut Sauce, Rosée Sauce, and Asian Sauce. I'll eat them with the authors.

"What should we bring? Wine? Dessert? Cheese?"

"I need new legs, a new back, a new brain."

That makes everyone laugh. It's like when I say: "That's sicker than I am." I'll tell the poets about my visit to Parc Safari. The lemurs had swollen bellies, like me. I joked around before. I said I was pregnant with the baby Jesus. It's the beginning of February and I still haven't given birth. The lemurs have no calendar. The joke can continue. The turkey didn't stop shrieking. Anatomy of my little sandwiches for the trip: rosemary ham, Dijon mustard, mayonnaise, and a lot of turkey. Ah. I scratched the belly of one of the male lemurs, singing a little tune. It was a spiritual moment. A little cry in the distance to spice up the moment. Oh. The turkey doesn't want to be forgotten.

I found a new stretch mark on my stomach. Baby Jesus is ready to come out. I'm ready too, but that stretch mark doesn't seem necessary. I named it Bertrand Vergeture. Ah. Give me a C-section for this water retention so I can be pretty like the girls in magazines. Give me an appointment. Ah. I've had enough of these stretch marks. I look at myself in the mirror. It looks like someone tried to chop me up. Shepherd's pie à la young girl. Oh. The poet friends freak out. They love how it's all meat, except my meat. They eat my sentences. At least they're good for something. The turkey likes that. Oh. The African porcupine wears a tutu. I'm alive. Each sentence is a feast.

A girl contacted me on Facebook. She'd heard about me and my love for fennec foxes. Her parents own Parc Safari. She invited me to come pet a baby fennec some afternoon.

There are so many nice people in the world. I'm the first to shout that it's full of dirtbags and lunatics watching Canal D on blast. I'm a VIP at the pharmacy and at Parc Safari. If you have a question for a doctor, I'll pass it on. I take care of everything. Drama queen. I met the fennec foxes. With my white crown, at Parc Safari. There are three. Mama, papa, and baby fennec. All nameless. They asked me for suggestions. For the parents, I thought of Eric and Lola. Legal proceedings take forever in Quebec. That will still be the case in a few years. Eric and Lola, the fennecs. Not bad. Nobody understands my obsession. Why these fennecs? Because they're cute. It's as simple as that. Why is your hair pink? Because it makes looking in the mirror more fun. When I'm sad, and the pink hair doesn't do it, I look at my pictures of Parc Safari. The baby fennec taking a nap in my scarf.

There is a literary life in Montreal. I like making trophies for the Gala of the Academy of Literary Life at the Turn of the XXI Century. If you publish a good book next year, you'll receive a foam hand. I'll be making faces on the ceiling. I dare to hope I'll be reincarnated as a butterfly. Special request. Britney Speaks will walk me on a leash. Expensive little butterfly. She'll hide me in a glass case at the botanical gardens. There'll be skulls with clouds on my wings. Custom. Or fennec foxes. Everyone asks me: "Why these foxes?" Why these questions? YouTube it. You'll spend the whole morning at it. You'll call me. We'll go to Parc Safari. When you see the baby, you'll freak out like the turkey. Ah. Oh. It'll inspire you to write poems. You'll write a whole collection. You'll call it *Melatonin*. I won't read the whole thing.

General observation on the current state of affairs
Instagram the nation
In bilingual French
I use complicated words
Cutting up my sentences
To be poetic
To think
I carry a little mirror in my purse
Fix yourself up with it
There are rocks and smog almost everywhere
Ghost town

Zombie mansion
Put on a little lipstick
Complete the ensemble

Mimosa Woolf

In one room, Anna Ketamine is doing a performance. She smokes a cigarette with a little half smile. On the cigarette, it says, *Happy After Poon*. A full pack and a little magnifying glass sit on a small table. The magnifying glass is a perfect circle of diamonds.

I wonder what the pussy of a plastic surgeon's daughter tastes like. My father is a plastic surgeon. My father is rich. Why are you telling me this? Why is it important? My father puts out forest fires. Your father and my father could talk about boobs. Yours and mine. Think about how much burned hair stinks. We won't introduce them to each other, thankfully. What does the pussy of a forest firefighter's daughter taste like? Tell me. Do our eyes have to bleed coke for us to claim we know about drugs? Can't we write a book about the life of an anonymous addict without ever touching drugs? I've done drugs. I don't write poems about snowbanks. I fall in them. Why am I here? I'm in Steph Liver's miniseries. My character is named Mimosa Woolf. My mother came up with the name. She knows I love Virginia. She saw me forget to eat while I was reading *The Waves*, skipping a whole generation of meals. I got dragged to a super-exclusive photo shoot this week. You have to write to be invited. I write, so I'm invited. They cut my shoes out of the shot. My mother is sad, they were her shoes. Why am I here? I can't say no. I'm always down for bad ideas. Try me, I always say yes. I dreamed that Samuel was a mermaid. I should maybe tell you about my dream. I could share intimate things too. Like my compulsion for deflowering men, or for sleeping with men who say absolutely nothing when I'm sad. Such sadness. I'm a soldier, I can do it. Pow pow agony. I will do none of this. I'll shout. Why am I here? Why can't I say no? Why the table? Why this corner? People leave their empty glasses on my table. There are always people in front of the projector. People should applaud. People put their things on my table. I'm supposed to write on this table. I have only one desire, to go to Sexe Cité across the street to buy things. And read the instructions, in a slightly amused but intense tone. Why am I here? Anna Ketamine is here, right next to me, thankfully. She whispers performance ideas to me. To remind me what it is. And to get me a drink. I'm good, I don't drink anymore. Just one drink, that's fine. I'm not going to write a masterpiece here. I'm going to get up soon to go read my text. But in the meantime, I'm sitting. I have to pee. I'd like to piss on the ground and dance like a crazy person to the electronic music on Mathieu's iPod. Waving around my pink dildo for emergencies. Trashy drama queen, yes. Why am I here? Anna Ketamine left. My dildo is in my bag, behind the little door to the administrative wing. Anna Ketamine left, why did Anna Ketamine leave? Why am I here? *Mise en abyme*, jargon wagon, a text that describes everything happening right before your eyes, right beneath your shoulders. I'm here at the perfect height for contemplating your asses. I'm in the back, in the corner. I have a projector.

It's keeping me warm. There's a girl with a striped sweater blocking half the words. Earlier, it was Laurence. There's always someone. I could ask Bertrand to squeeze over. I know him. I know a lot of people. I'd have another drink. Or forty. Why am I here? When I went to the bathroom I noticed that you can see through my leggings a little. I was going to tell you about my G-string but you already know. I also noticed that the thing I use to make a living is still whole. My pussy is no longer a pussy, it's a fennec fox. The boy that I love is fucking a girl in the room. I don't know who it is either. Don't hurt your neck. I could talk about it. I'm trying to stop. Why am I here? We're working on a super-trendy collaboration with just girls. We're going to strap on a penis and express our femininity. Libertine baguettes. I still haven't found a title. I'm working on it. I'm working on a lot of things. I'm always busy. Too busy even to hold my mic. Claudine just arrived. She's beautiful. I'm going to compliment her and offer her my coat. Do you want to be part of our collaboration, Claudine? You're wearing my coat and you're beautiful. Why am I here? I'm also working on this top-secret project with only people from Generation Y. We're going to photocopy everyone's birth certificates. Super exclusive. You, Anna Ketamine, you do performance art, you could definitely get in on this. You have your birth certificate, right? We're renting a giant martini glass and we'll put you in it. You speak Finnish, nobody understands, it's like you're vodka personified. People get up, applaud, and leave the room. Why am I here? Oh. That there is for you. We're going to organize a round table on Generation Y, yes, and you'll be in the corner. You're going to write in the corner. We'll put you on an overhead projector to be fancy. You'll read your text at the end. You told the guys from Poème Sale that you'd write a poem. So, you wrote:

I have balsamic vinaigrette on my hands
Claudine is beautiful
That's all there is to say

INTERMISSION AT THE WAX MUSEUM

VICTORIA LOVE

Maggie is bringing us to the wax museum. I'm going for the literary section. The architecture of the building is unique. It's a triangle. Like the musical instrument or Laughing Cow cheese. I'm going to see Josée Yvon in a wax tutu. Otherwise I wouldn't be interested. My wheelchair would make their day more complicated, for nothing. Apparently they have Marie-Soleil Tougas and Ève Cournoyer in wax too. I don't know. Seems to me there's a lack of accessories. If Ève was dressed as a sushi girl, I'd freak out. If they put Marie-Soleil in an astronaut suit, I'd rejoice.

ANNA KETAMINE

I'm still wondering why I said yes. I always say yes. I'm useful, I push the chair. I have no shortage of suffering friends. I don't want to stay till the end. I've done all my performances. I've done everything to help Victoria Love. I'm not staying for the depressing parts. I'll push the chair, and after the museum, it's over.

Josée Yvon in a tutu

The face of a medusa.

For the face: the front of a car. The headlights are the eyes.
The nose should be the thing the City puts on the wheels
of your car when you don't pay your parking tickets. You
know, the yellow thing.

For the snake hair: plastic dildos in girly colours, like lesbian
strap-ons. Giant vacuum tubes.

On the adjacent wall: Barbie dolls in two colours, black
and white. A portrait of society. Barbie dolls with different
clothing styles. Barbie dolls in all colours stuck to a strip of
flypaper.

It's Valentine's Day. Last Saturday, I went to see *Pleasure Dome* at Agora de la danse. One of the dancers was giving out little chocolate hearts. I didn't get one. I sulked for five minutes. Valentine's Day is everywhere, even at contemporary dance shows. Sometimes I like going to shows even when they're getting bad reviews, just for the nudity. It's the complete opposite of voyeurism. I calibrate my eyes. I look around, no beige. The black of the curtain and the floor. Velvet. An almost luxurious black. Sometimes it gives the impression that the darkness, that everything dangerous and opaque about the world, is a burden we can do nothing about. The dancer arches his shoulders back toward the floor, flows down onto it like lava. The other dancer is lying on the floor, or in a heap, her body jerking as if she's convulsing. But there is always, in every show, a moment, *the* moment. Regardless of the choreographer's intentions, there is always at least one moment. The male dancer quivers, he makes large movements, like he's flying, quickly getting up to stretch his arms to the sky, bending them a little to gain momentum and then turning around, spinning, rolling in a ball from one side of the stage to the other to get up, clutching his stomach with his forearms, the face of a cherub. The black spaces are now ringed in beige, a sparkling beige, a luminous beige, everything that a life that continues contains, promises of a day or a moment of pure happiness, happiness that makes you forget everything else, that justifies the journey, the dirty, rocky road that leads to the vanishing point. I need to turn my brain off sometimes, to perform my duty of contemplating the world, without processing the smallest piece of data, to put the algebra of my right iris to sleep, to have no more function than an object, a Tupperware, a bowl of fruit, a hook, to simply contain. The hand of the clock for a metronome. Just shaking my head. Like algae at the mercy of the currents. In the same vein, to fulfill that same need for mental vacation: American television, chick flicks, reality TV about the fashion world, and paintings of fields of flowers. When I'm depressed I like going to the Musée des beaux-arts to look at the most mundane paintings of daisies, the little botanical garden, the walls like the pages of a picture book. Need to remind myself that things used to be beautiful and simple. Without pretention. Only need to be alive and standing. Right now, I think you're my dance show, you're my field of wild strawberries, my little pot of jam, my little plot of soil. Little lace curtain for existence. Little wisp of steam from the teapot, little opera in my thatched cottage. Little prince in my bookshelf. I like it when things are two colours. Ink on paper: two colours. Black-and-white sentences. I stare. The dancers when they're naked. Their shadow, if they cast one. I stare at Karine. Little vixen. I look more like the other dancer caught in her wires. She's on all fours. You can't fall down from all fours. Perfect for me. Hello, catharsis.

The new feature of my illness is Jell-O legs. Especially at night and in the morning. Getting out of bed is a challenge. I try to give myself some momentum to scale the mountain of blankets. It's a repetitive movement. You picture it, you know what it makes you think of. Especially when I sleep naked. Horn dog. You turn on the light and change your mind. The girl has skin like soft marble because of her stretch marks. The girl is on a soft-foods diet. You can tell just by looking at her. The girl is sick. One year ago, you paid the girl to take off her bra. Now you'd pay her to put it back on. Her hands. Her hands smell like shit. She gives you your twenty-dollar bill. The bill smells like her hands. The odour is contagious. She explains that she has a hard time wiping herself, taking other bills out of her purse. She pays you to listen. The bills are brown. You are her therapist.

My therapist wanted me to tell him about my dreams. I told him: it's really boring. I dream about food. The food I'm going to eat the next day. I explain everything in my books. The therapist just has to read my book. That's what it's for. Ten books in one. I went to the hospital this morning. For my appointment with my other therapist, a woman. I like her better. She's not mystical or superstitious. And she has two arms. You judge the male therapist because he only has one arm. Hey, I slept with a one-legged guy once, I've done my part. I came home in a taxi. Big spender. The warmth feels good. It took me an hour to get home from the therapist's office. The hours fly. Time moves quickly in the life of a sick person. I have no problem donating my hours. To science, to the cafeteria where I eat lunch to pass the time. But words, that hurts. I have almost none left. Words, often the same ones, until the supply runs out. Every day, I have to say it: I'm going to die, my tumour is back, I only have a few months left. The last time, my mother was in charge of telling everyone. I'd given her the numbers of my friends. *Ring, ring,* get to the hospital. The friend, the tears, the little collaborative poem with a mistake in my name. I only remember the bits Anna Ketamine wrote. She was the only one in the collaborative poem who wasn't a poet. It says a lot about my love of the genre.

Watching the clouds calms me down. I always loved clouds, looking for shapes in them. The sky is a collection of poetry. Every time I go to the drugstore, I think about the poem by Frédéric Dumont. He was going to buy a bird at the drugstore. I go to the drugstore often. They don't sell birds. But poetry's kind of like that. Maybe I'm wrong. Maybe I'm just in the mood for some St-Hubert chicken.

Everyone who lives in a studio apartment writes at least one poem in their meagre little existence. They get attached to the poem like it's a talisman. Dumont doesn't live in a studio apartment. I've been to his house. There were books all over the floor. I waited for him while he went to the drugstore. I slept for fifteen minutes among the books. I wrote this little poem when I woke up:

I asked them to show me the baby at my
    second abortion to traumatize myself
I got a third abortion
No ketchup
Won't work
Hungry
For good blood sausage

I have a big fucking ego. Tell me not to do something, I am obviously going to do it. When I want to burp or fart, I go to the table before I let it out. I cracked a beer the day before my first intravenous chemo. Well no, doctor, I didn't listen to you. There's a good chance this won't work. There's a good chance I'll die. Might as well do so with a stupid grin on my face.

I dreamed I had an autistic sister. I was helping her choose a job. She was deciding between Winners and the homemade beeswax candle shop. A job for the holidays. I had an idea in my dream, the first time that's happened. Maybe it happens all the time and I just never remember: I could dye chickens to make earrings.

I decided I was going to live ten years and write ten books. For the ten years, fail. But nothing's stopping me from writing ten books. The other day, I was flipping channels. The universe winked at me. Yes, that motherfucker. A man was wearing an orange jacket over a purple T-shirt. My next book will be orange. No. It'll be rainbow! Like the fish in the children's book. I dream in colour. I want to see everything, visualize everything before I go. Yesterday was hard. I went shopping. I bought myself a cute green shoulder bag with studs. It's depressing to think about all that. If I can buy a smaller purse it's because I don't need to keep papers in it anymore. No more blood-test forms, no more appointment forms, no more parking tickets from the hospital.

Yesterday I gave away all my clothes. Two big green bags. Linda, the nurse who helps me shower, left with one big bag. She has a sixteen-year-old daughter. I love Linda. She understands that "How are you?" makes me sick. My mother's friend Maryse left with the other bag. Two big bags full of clothes worn once or twice. So many colours. Green is supposed to be the colour of imagination. The yellow roses I was given are supposed to represent infidelity. I'm not faithful to my menu. I watch videos of food I can't eat because of the drugs I'm taking. No beans, no cheese, nothing aged, no alcohol, no charcuterie. There are a lot of foods on the blacklist. I can only eat four things. I feel like Sophy, Mathieu's vegetarian girlfriend. Sometimes I open the fridge and daydream. What could I eat? What will my mother cook tonight? It's a nice activity. I can't eat cheese, no prosciutto. I make a list of the foods I can't eat anymore. I can write them down, that's something at least. I open the fridge. I survey the little cheese drawer. I whisper sweet nothings to it. Then I go sit on the couch. I indulge in shows about food I can't have. I act like when I have to fast. A little masochistic. I pet my cookie in the dim living room. I tell it sweet things, I promise it I'll eat it. Cookies like being eaten. I don't understand why *cookie* isn't a feminine word in French.

I'll have a crown.
I'll go to New York.
My friend Daniel says he'll marry me.
I'll be able to strike things off my bucket list.
When I go to New York,
I'll go by water like Godzilla.
Trampling down everything in my way with my huge tail.
Or my big tutu.
Maggie is coming for supper tonight.
We're going to eat quail in port.
She's going to give me one of her film descriptions
    in little chandeliers.

Starbuck and the Powerless

A GASPAR NOÉ FILM

Marie-Soleil Tougas is wearing Lolita sunglasses.
Heart-shaped, they look like they were made from candy.
Super close-up: yes, from candy cane, no glass, wink.
She's walking with a big bright green latte from Starbucks.
This film is in colour. We're on Coloniale, she's heading
south, walking like a girl still drunk from the night before.
A bit wobbly. Pass a father pushing his son in a baby
carriage. A blue carriage with a white stain, definitely ice
cream, on the canopy. As if the father made a mess at the
park. Marie-Soleil spills her boiling coffee on the child.
Next shot: it's night. Tons of journalists are taking her
photo: the girl who killed a child with her hot coffee.
The scene is not for epileptics. Little travelling shot:
in the hands of all the paramedics, photographers, police
officers, a bright green Starbucks coffee.

THE END

Marie-Soleil Tougas

The queen of the whole show, the pièce de résistance. A
forest of animal parts. Trees of chicken feet and cat feet. A
goat-horn lawn with parrot-head flowers. A path that cuts
the forest in two. At the end, a tower, like Rapunzel's tower:
a boar paw on which sits the body of a faceless girl, plain
beige, her eyes two stitched Xs like on teddy bears. A curly
pig's tail lies on the ground.

The pig's tail is covered in pink gemstones.

Candles and flowers on the threshold of the room, a bit
like when someone dies in shocking, unfair circumstances.
Everyone is carrying photos of Marie-Soleil Tougas, paper
lanterns, flowers, and messages of hope. It's your favourite
part of the exhibition. I understand. It made me sad too.
We're going to talk about it all together. We're going to have
a little more fiction. Seems it's good for the soul.

I have AIDS.
I have hepatitis A.
I have hepatitis B.

I'm going to hang myself.
I'm going to open my veins.
I'm going to throw myself off an overpass.

I have suicidal thoughts.
The baby is crying.
I hope I'm clean.

I'm writing a novel.
You're reading it.
We have a relationship.

I have to describe shocking things.
I have to keep you on the edge of your seat.

I have to split your heart in two.
Take you by the hand.
Dear reader.

Want me to make you something to eat?
If not, why would you have come over with a bottle of
    wine?
You want us to eat together.
For me to take your life in my hands.
Dear reader.

The table is set for you and me.
Another table is set for two nearby.
I ask you to help me pull it over to ours.
We are waiting for people, important people.
Dear reader.

You have to recognize yourself somewhere.
I have to tell you about things you know.
But also things you don't know,
    that exist only in my head.
It has to be like a melody,
    this literature.
Dear reader.

You must never forget that I am like you.
Nobody.
An individual, with a last name and a publisher,
    sure, but above all, nobody.
Dear reader.

I spilled my hot coffee on a living child.
I spilled my hot coffee on a living baby.
I spilled my coffee on a baby.

I want to have a baby. A baby without all the responsibilities.
I want to raise someone else's child. The stretch marks, the
weight, none of that would bother me too much, but the
responsibilities are another story. I kill all my plants. I have
no ID cards. I haven't had a bank card in three years, I go to
Insta-Cheques when I have a cheque to deposit, I don't care
about the three per cent they take. I'm too punk to have a
kid. And besides, I'd have to get my IUD taken out and fuck
a fertile guy without a condom. A smart guy who will still
fuck a near stranger without a condom, like a smart, normal
guy. All the guys around me are smart. I'm part of a cerebral
scene. It won't be hard to find someone. But I don't want
the responsibilities. I flee responsibility. I don't clean up my
room. I'm fucking twenty-three years old and I don't pick
up my dirty dishes. The DNA would be good, progeny and
all that. But the heartbreak, the shame when I leave. Because
I'm going to end up leaving. We're all going to die, but this
is different. I'm going to leave, I know it.

I want to create an object of beauty. I want to offer everything I am in a single sentence, put myself on a silver platter,
on all fours, all wet, but I am nothing.

I am in the hall of my château.
I am in the baby section at Rossy.
I am at the grocery store.

I am at the grocery store. I need milk, sugar cereal, and yo-gourt. My sister is not dead yet but might as well be. She's coming back home for a few days. She has to put her pills in yogourt to swallow them. The sugar cereal is a whim. For my mother and me, none of Victoria Love's requests are whims. She's going to die, she has the right to be demanding, to ask for anything she pleases during her ephemeral passage here on earth. I am all alone in the grocery store. There are a lot of people, the line must be long, but I feel like I'm alone and the solitude feels good. Everything is heavy. The milk, the cereal, the atmosphere in the house.

I write autofiction.
I write fiction.
Which is better?
Don't answer right away.
Let's play.

My name is Marie-Antoinette.
My sister's name is Victoria Love.
My mother's name is Alice.

My first boyfriend's name was David.
Victoria Love's first boyfriend's name was David.

My first cat's name was Snowflake and he was black.
My sister's first cat's name was Snowflakes
    and he was spotted.

When Marie-Soleil Tougas died in a tragic plane crash, my sister's life turned upside down. Drama queen nearly tearing her hair out. She spent hours crouched in front of the television, watching people come together. All those people promising to never forget her. With their big signs, their big flower arrangements. In under two minutes, there were commemorative candles, key chains, posters, party hats. On TV, they showed people making piles of objects bearing her photo to demonstrate their sorrow. The television station dedicated a whole afternoon to her, a whole day, they were going to stretch it out over a week if necessary. Marie-Soleil was the Princess Diana of Quebec. Victoria Love, my mother, and me, we were nobody, we would stay nobody, we would all three of us pass through this life as nobody, but Marie-Soleil, she'd managed to be someone, someone important. Tons of people who'd never met her in real life, in the flesh, thousands of people were weeping for her. She'd made it.

Victoria Love perched on the pouf in the living room staring at the box of images, fascinated. I was helping my mother do the dishes in exchange for another orange cookie. Maman asked Victoria Love to turn it down. She turned it up. Marie-Antoinette Love is my name. Victoria Love is my sister's name. They call her Love. She had to start somewhere if she wanted to be someone. She had to start by dominating one person, then little Quebec, the States, then the whole world, the whole universe by the end. The universe. Marie-Antoinette to start. Me. Weaker though older, a simple defenceless girl. My little sister was never gentle with me. I've been followed, hunted my entire life.

The nickname came just like that. My mother always took us camping in Brébeuf during the construction holiday. I had a little seasonal boyfriend. Every summer, we'd make out to the sound of the crackling campfire and I'd get some great stories to tell my friends back at school. I exaggerated, like any self-respecting teenager. I made him more gorgeous than he actually was. His name was David, people called him Dave. He had a mole with two little hairs just above his right eyebrow. I never drew the mole when I doodled hearts and flowers all around his face for the curious eye of the girl who sat next to me at school. Victoria Love drew the mole. It was the summer of Marie-Soleil. My sister stole my little boyfriend. She lifted her pencil, she started by drawing the mole, then she carefully drew the hairs, made them meet, arched in the shape of a heart. She insisted on calling him David. It made him feel like he was someone. Everything might have been different if I'd kept calling him David. Left for a younger girl, for my own sister. The drama. My friends at school were outraged. But I mostly just found David boring. He only had four topics of conversation. He was too into my face. His hands shook all the time. He came to visit Love one winter day. He hadn't done that for me. I should say that David lived in Rimouski. We were big-city girls. The big city is scary for small-town people. That winter, David's parents came up for the holidays. An aunt was going to die, they had to make an appearance, they'd promised the grandfather on his deathbed. They were always saying they were principled people who keep their word out there in the quiet wood. It was time to prove it. So David came to visit Love during the holidays. It was brief. He came and went quickly, like a thief. His parents were doing the round trip to deliver the obligatory chocolates. David and Love shut themselves in her room. I was helping Maman set the table. I was wearing an apron with gingerbread snowmen on it. Double Christmas. Joël Legendre was on TV in the kitchen. Joyeux Noël, Soyeux Joël. Maman never turns on that TV. There's too much static. It's mainly there for decoration. David was already coming back out of the room. He was standing in front of me. Bye, Merry Christmas. He was going to get my name wrong, he freaked out, he catapulted the two into one, his head a metronome ticking between us. Love. It stuck.

She always did her best to show me everything I could have been. It was subtle. She started by getting a haircut like mine. Then it was her nails. I always did two fingers of my right hand in a different colour than the rest. She did three. And so on and so forth, always one better. When even my mother started calling her Love, I gave up. I did what any girl with heavy emotional baggage and no self-respect would do, I started doing drugs, fucking strangers, slowly destroying myself. To make my life bearable, to help me swallow it all down.

VICTORIA LOVE

They call me Love. It drives my sister crazy. She's a little older. A year and change. I'm twenty-two, she's twenty-three. Our birthdays are in spring. Our mother makes an amazing raspberry upside-down cake. We celebrate everything at the same time. Mother's Day, our birthdays. It often falls on the week of my birthday. Every year our mother ends up telling the story of how I was conceived in Venezuela. That's what you get with a tipsy mother. She tells stories. She never tells the story of Marie-Antoinette's conception. Makes you wonder if my mother was tipsy when she conceived the living thing that is my sister and she doesn't remember anymore. I prefer it when people call me Victoria. It pisses my sister off less.

That was fiction.
This is not true and my name is not Bertolt Brecht.
What does that make me?
An author or a liar?

Are you angry?
Do you feel duped?
Are you sick of hearing about my illness?
Did you read my other book?
Do you know that I have cancer?
You find that heavy, hey?

We'll keep going a little longer.
I have more ideas.
I'll write short paragraphs, promise.
I'll stop talking about my illness too.
If I can. I'll try really, really hard.

MARIE-ANTOINETTE LOVE

Our mother brought us to the florist. The man is taking his time. He's in a trance, with white lilies in one hand and yellow daisies in the other. My mother comes to see him every week. He's usually on time. This arrangement is more difficult. Since she opened her breakfast place, she gets floral arrangements every week to decorate the window, always tied in with the menu. It's Thursday night, it's bedtime. Love and I are whining. We know we'll have to go by the restaurant to decorate the window before bed. There are steps before the pyjamas. It's difficult to arrange a sunny-side-up egg out of flowers. We're too little and too tired to be understanding. The man offers to let each of us choose a plant, to reward us for our patience. I choose an African violet and Love a kind of fancy fern that looks like angel hair.

My African violet never flowered.
Neither did Love's fern.
My mother will go bankrupt because of the economy.

She hasn't been at the same location since. She managed to start a little chain of restaurants based on her concept, but her golden years are definitely behind her. It's over. It's all over.

Maggie invites me out for a beer.
Or several.
That's how she put it in the text message.

Elevator to the Hot Folds

A LOUIS MALLE FILM

The elevator can hold no more than fifteen people.
Otherwise it stops, like in the real movie. Who am I
inviting to my party? Dakota, Lise, and Renée, for sure.
I'm inviting myself. It's my party. I invite Benjamin even
though that's complicated. Marie-Antoinette, because
it's crazy fun having parties with a bunch of people with
loaded pasts. Put all the underage people in a pile and
pour vodka right into their mouths. With fur hats so big
they count as people. Big cotton balls. I have two spots
left for two people with big hats. All the hats must meow
and be white. I'll put an ad on Craigslist. Seeking Ilsa, She
Wolf of the SS, and her whole crew.

THE END

Victoria Love

Against a large wall, in a spacious room, an enormous nose with a clip. A silver piercing in the nose in the shape of a gun.

An explosion of blood hangs in the emptiness directly below the gun piercing.

The bullet of the gun slips out of the blood explosion: it's a silver penis.

I am a stripper.
I am a florist.
I am a saleswoman in a furniture store.

I sell furniture you pay for in installments. My life is boring.
My job holds no potential for fantasy. I try to finish early so
I can go see Harmony Korine's last film at Fantasia. But no,
the boss doesn't want to hear it.

I am an agent of luxury.
I am a technician of floral arrangements.
I am an administrative assistant.

I was a dancer. I wonder if that's relevant to mention. If
everyone absolutely has to know to understand my world.
I'm not a prude. I'm comfortable with and in my body. I've
always respected myself.

There, see, I'm mixing fiction and autofiction.

Is that bad?

Can I write in the grey area like that?

I'm definitely asking too many questions.

You pick up the book and you think, *Ah, here is someone other than myself,* but this someone doesn't stop questioning you, it can be annoying.

Put down the book.

Go on, put it down.

I'm sorry.

Pick it back up.

Let's continue.

I turn the oven up to three fifty but I open it first to make sure it's empty. Sometimes my mother leaves croutons in there to dry.

I'm talking about my real mother here. She really does that.

The oven is empty and set at three hundred and fifty degrees. I put in the seafood lasagna in rosée sauce that I made for my birthday.

I actually made a seafood lasagna in rosée sauce for my birthday for real.

Nobody came, nobody ever comes, I have no friends, nobody wants me. I'm whining a lot today.

There were actually about fifteen people who came, I'm exaggerating. I was depressed when I wrote that. Even though being depressed is something living people do. Ah, I promised I wouldn't talk about my illness anymore.

Put it down again.
I'm sorry.
Let's continue.

There are a lot of leftovers. I put them in the freezer. I look at myself in the oven window. I'm vain. I look at myself in mirrors when I go to dinner parties, in the mirrors behind the seats when I'm in a backroom with a client, in car windows, in shop windows. I put my makeup on in taxis and hired cars. I'm dangerous. I see no more than you do. I see myself with my eyes but mostly with my head. My head says I'm not pretty anymore and nobody wants me. I sit near the oven to feel waves of unbearable heat. On purpose.

So everything is true in this text up till now, except for the oven. I reheated my lasagna at three hundred and fifty when Mathieu came to take care of me. I won't tell you why he came to take care of me. We said we wouldn't talk about it anymore. But he came to my birthday and he asked for seconds so I thought it would be nice to reheat it for him. I did it. I just didn't do it all alone and in the way I said. Does that take away the flavour? Because I could do it for real. I could certainly sit in front of a three-hundred-and-fifty-degree oven with my computer to type these lines.

There, it's done.

I'm sitting cross-legged in front of the oven,
    bent over my computer.
The oven is at three-fifty and there are
    no croutons inside.
What am I doing now?
You want me to share some intimate details?
OK.
I'll break your heart.
Dear reader.

Talk to you about sex. About my sex life. About how depressing it is since the thing we are not talking about. It's been a long time since I wanted it. We'll do it together. Phallic vegetables. Oh yes, we're going there. Already. My body is wrecked. I'm going to insert vegetables inside it, yes, and we're going to do it together. Already. We're intimate, very intimate. My mother isn't here. She had a doctor's appointment and a date with a guy named Benoît. If she asks me what I ate for dinner, I'll tell her vegetable soup. I'll lie to my mother for now. You're my witness. She'll read my book and find out that her carrot ended up in my ass. I'll leave the new potatoes even though they'd make not bad ben wa balls. We were planning to make shepherd's pie tomorrow. It should be a piece of cake for you. I don't understand why they always say that when something's easy. Making a cake is not easy. You have to do it in steps. There's the homemade ganache. Sometimes fruit jelly. Decorations with a piping bag.

Do you have to cut off an ear? Do you have to self-immolate?

I'm going to shove a carrot up my ass.
I'm going to make an effort.

It'll be a piece of cake for me. Carrot cake. Like the one I bought Mathieu for his birthday at the café in the metro. He almost cried when he found it waiting for him in the fridge. The little square of carrot cake. Philadelphia cream cheese. I have all the ingredients at home. You open my fridge and freak out. All the ingredients of a winning recipe. A piece of cake.

I'll never again wake up in someone's arms. Unless I pay them. Everything has a price. Everything can be bought. But I come with big suitcases. Full cargo. And a cat soon enough. My mother is going to end up saying yes. Because I live with my mother now. Fixed address and everything. I'm going to call the cat Gâteau. In Italian, cat is *gatto*. I'm always hungry. Especially for dessert. Gâteau my little cake cat. I think that's funny. My uncle would make some joke about how he's not going to eat it, he's not Vietnamese. Crack himself up. There was a contestant on *Come Dine with Me* who talked like that. I found it so depressing. We look like a bunch of idiots to the rest of the world. We: Great Nation, the Québécois. TV is important. It's like Barbies and douchebags, you can't talk about it too long. It makes you look silly. Can I just say that I find turtlenecks ugly? Super ugly. You can't talk about that too long either. If you have a puppy to name, think about that guy who got stuck in the woods. He had to eat his. It was called Ti-Concombre. Little cucumber. It was written in the stars that he would eat it.

You can't talk about a dog named Ti-Concombre without thinking about eating it. OK, my story to break your heart is not working. I'm too busy to break your heart. I'll insert vegetables into my orifices later. For now, I'll continue my novel, our novel of us, because I have nothing better to do.

My name is Marie-Antoinette.
I speak to you in the third person.
About my ghosts, about my vegetables.

Marie-Antoinette is an activist. She's done crazy things. She was the one behind the stretcher coup. Everywhere. In all the hospitals of the world. All the stretchers with indulgent victims. Each one bearing the red square. From the stretcher of the grumpy old man to the one with the young hillbilly. The stretchers all tipped over at the same time. Her sister is in the hospital; she had to cheer her up, make her laugh. Her laugh was like the ocean's laugh. A mocking little laugh. So cute. The stretcher coup is going to go down in history. The population says that's OK. The people's money goes to sick people, to health. Good. We need that money. We're sick. Being sick sucks and it hurts. Assisted suicide.

Yesterday, Marie-Antoinette got drunk. With her friend Maggie. She met her at Bar Inc. around nine. They met some journalists from Radio-Canada. There are journalists everywhere. These ones all work for *La Presse*. They also like V-neck shirts. They came over. They bought shots. The night continued elsewhere with more drinks. At one of their places. His name was Joseph and it was on his couch that Marie-Antoinette woke up. She hadn't slept much. They'd gotten Peter to come for her. She still had the *Drive* sound-track and too much Drake in her ears. Joseph's place was not far from Saint-Joseph. Marie-Antoinette showed him her right breast when they were on the street the next morning. Maggie wanted to buy a powder puff and her Dove shampoo so they went to Familiprix on the corner of Laurier and Saint-Denis. Marie-Antoinette showed Joseph her breast as they crossed Saint-Joseph. Some kids saw. Oops. On the way to the breakfast place. With the bag from the pharmacy full of stupid stuff. They stopped in a pet shop to buy a leash. Maggie bought stuff for her bag and her happiness. Chocolate, buttons, and stuff that makes noise. She immediately attached the leash to Peter's jeans. Marie-Antoinette had spent the night in Peter's arms. He'd said he had a girlfriend at home. He was supposedly noble and faithful. At breakfast, they order a half-litre of white wine. That kind of morning. Marie-Antoinette goes to call her mother. Her mother will tell her that her sister has disappeared. Marie-Antoinette already knows this, but she won't tell her mother where she is. Love is bathing in American waters, Maman. It's no use. She is far away and alone, that's what's important. She'd escaped the hospital. Marie-Antoinette had helped her. She'd put her sister on a bus and went to meet Maggie so she'd have an alibi. Maggie had been waiting with a bucket of green beers. They'd met the journalists out smoking on the patio. Joseph had understood some of Marie-Antoinette's references. She'd borrowed these ideas from her sister. In any case. They've just gone into the breakfast place. Maggie doesn't take off her coat. She plays with her iPhone. She's popular, that girl. Maggie still hasn't hung her coat on the hook. Night comes quickly. Maggie leaves and asks Marie-Antoinette to call her later. She leaves with the results of their strip Scrabble party from the night before. She's proud. She's right to be. Marie-Antoinette stays. Peter also stays for the movie. A Jean-Claude Van Damme movie. Marie-Antoinette promises to call Maggie. They go into the living room. Jean-Claude full frontal. It really is just a little movie about Jean-Claude's big cock. Marie-Antoinette wonders if he actually has a big cock. Enrique Iglesias has a small cock. He said so himself at a show. He launched a collection of small condoms specially designed for his cause.

You wouldn't know it, but it was a big day for Marie-Antoinette. Maggie was a bad influence. It had started innocently enough when Marie-Antoinette had called her mother. She was freaking out. Maggie had said: "Your mother's driving you crazy, come meet me." She didn't need to be asked twice. Everyone seemed more understanding than her mother. Marie-Antoinette had gotten too drunk. She'd told the whole story, unloaded it all: "My sister's going to die. They opened up her head. There was nothing more they could do. It's spread too far. She found an architect who designed a Euthanasia Coaster. I put her on a bus just now. She wants to meet the architect. My mother is going to keep crying. She sees herself as a solute for the world. Super melodramatic. It rubs off on me a little with alcohol, I guess. I tell myself that it's normal to absorb it. These are difficult days. I'm overflowing, getting myself all worked up." Now Marie-Antoinette arrives at Alexandre's place in a taxi. Maggie gives her amphetamines and puts on Skrillex.

It's a bit heavy. Guillaume is sitting in a corner. He showers Marie-Antoinette in awkward compliments. Maggie had suggested a foursome. She needed an excuse to sleep with Alexandre again. He's her ex. A bit of a jerk. But whatever, apparently he has a big dick like Jean-Claude. Marie-Antoinette is too sad to judge. Guillaume will do like Peter did yesterday. At Joseph's, they'd used Peter's ass as a DVD player. At least it was funny with him. It's going to take more wine and a poker party for Guillaume to do it. A lot of wine and a lot of cigarettes. Even the dubstep seems pointless. They really need more wine. Guillaume goes to get some red with Maggie. Marie-Antoinette gives Alexandre a blow job. Since they're there, and naked or close to naked. A blow job to pass the time. "Good thing I can play DJ," Marie-Antoinette thinks aloud. A bit of Massive Attack, her mouth full. It adds a little something sensual. Marie-Antoinette would never in a million years have agreed to participate in this kind of night before. The time for prudishness is over. Maggie comes back with Guillaume. Hello, red wine. Very welcome in scratchy throats. Guillaume does the helicopter with his dick. The joke dies. To top it off, he's soft. Marie-Antoinette is too pretty. Even compared to her sister, she's curvier, more sensual, more charming.

This novel is about illness.
This novel is about the worst foursome ever.
But I can tell you about that another time.
Let's kill this novel.
You'll see, it'll be fun.

The characters are colourful, but it's confusing, this story about Love, who is in fact me. It's cute, but it loses the reader, it doesn't make any friends. Pow pow in the pile. So yes, novel, hang yourself with the L from Love so we can be done with it. Leave us, novel. Go find another book, see if I follow. I won't touch you again, not even with a ten-foot pole. You disgust me. You stink.

OK, I'm getting childish.
The third person has that effect on me.
I don't know anymore how many novels
    I've written and then destroyed.
I'm a serial killer of novels.
A man will come into my life and change everything.
I need a new man for my new life.
Let's invite the one who just came into the restaurant
    to our table.
Marie-Antoinette wakes up.
She wipes the bloodstain on her forehead.
She motions to him.
I'll let them chat at the table.
Get to know each other.
As if they were two actors I was hiring
    for my show.
Maggie and Marie-Antoinette.

Vain

Luka Rococo Magneto meets Nelly Arcan
in an empty, secluded pool hall out in the sticks. She
dances around the pole at their table as if it
were a strip club. Festival of Flirts. She laps at the pole.
It tastes salty, like bar peanuts. She makes a face.
Magneto too. It reminds them both of sperm.
A complicit little laugh. Magneto doesn't need to taste
it to know. He's gay, he knows. We can trust him. After-
partyin his Jacuzzi. Go. Next shot: Magneto pulls out
his victim's veinsand tries to hang her with them. It
works. Because it's a picture. Everything is possible at the
pictures. The film makes you want to eat Black Forest
cake. With your hands. Which you do.

THE END

Ève Cournoyer

At the entrance to the room: a warning. Not recommended for epileptics. An enormous bra. With patterned fabric: spray-paint the bodies in black on the skeleton stencil and make a circle with red spray for the heads.

Stroboscopes, behind the two "breasts," that form the nipples.

Studs everywhere on the contours of the bra (full of silver metallic objects, like mini Christmas trees and sparkling garlands, funnels, spider head massagers).

I'm going to Marie-Antoinette's in Sainte-Agathe
to write.
I'm going to Marie-Antoinette's in Sainte-Agathe
to do nothing.
We end up doing nothing the whole time.
Almost a week.
Of my time alive.
Several days of doing absolutely nothing except
watching TV and hanging around the house.
Chilling with my stepmother, Catherine.
Our father got remarried.
Marie-Antoinette followed him.
Catherine is cool but I prefer my roots,
my love mother.
I come spend a week here sometimes.
To talk about her cancer, mine, writing, the people
she serves in her restaurant.
More illness.

One in two people has cancer.
We both have it.
A couple of miracles around the same table.

We make a cake from a box mix.
We make a pecan cake with
    butter-cream icing.
We make a cake.

We ate the rest of the butter-cream icing with our fingers right from the bowl. Not in slow motion but almost. We were American. We licked our fingers like Americans. I need to describe this house to you since you're coming with me. I'm not holding you prisoner, you can always leave, but I swear it's going to get interesting. You shouldn't miss the part of the movie with the explosions because you needed to pee. Good things come to those who know how to be patient. I'm the first one to get up to whine, start losing my shit, my pretty little shit, but the universe doesn't care about these cute things, these little nothings getting all excited. The universe doesn't care about the number of pages I blacken before starting to entertain you. The universe would be just as satisfied if I kept you up at night telling you about the consistency of my shit in alexandrine verse. That's kind of what I'm doing already. I'm relating the circumstances. This morning, my shit smelled like merguez. This afternoon, I took the longest piss in the world. Not in the bath this time. I like pissing in the bath. Mostly to talk about it. A photo for Instagram. The photos need a caption to really shine. Otherwise it's a pretty ordinary account. Photos of food, photos of me naked in the bath with a little tuft of bubbles over my pussy.

So, I was saying: the house. It's rectangular, it has two floors and a basement, a cat named Ti-Loup, an oven that doesn't heat like other ovens. What are we doing? Why are we waiting at the kitchen table? Well, because no ovens ever heat like other ovens. The crazy things you're expecting me to tell you about all happen in the most boring and ordinary places. It's here, in this house in Sainte-Agathe-des-Monts, out in the Laurentian Mountains, that I'll turn into a fairy for the first time. I'm not like other fairies. I'm a fairy who gives a shit. A noble fairy. Not a little girl in a costume. I put on my nightgown up in the bedroom and it starts itching my back. It burns my spine. A stream of lava. I'm like the Hulk, but the girl version.

I'm a queen.
I'm a fairy.
I'm fasting.

This morning I'm a fairy. Since yesterday I've been a fairy. We feel good. We have faces full of diamonds. We have voices like little bells. Sleepy little eyes because of too much coke yesterday. I wrote high yesterday. I had a little leftover in my wallet. I wanted to write and my stepmother was deep in a red-wine sleep. My little brother was upstairs with his friend who looks like him. The house was essentially deserted. The perfect moment for writing, but the inspiration still wouldn't come. So I turned back to my old friend in its little bag. I said to it: "Make me a fairy." I wrote texts I was ashamed of when I looked at them this morning. I'm always ashamed of having written intoxicated. I hide my fairy texts. I'm ashamed of them. Like my visual arts projects. My scrapbook, my decoration project, the trepanned mirror. I only half commit to them. I can see you're disappointed.

I'm a queen when I drink to write. My meal is a feast. My iTunes, an orchestra. My headphones, a stage. I could publish the most excessive notebooks, I have so much stuff lying around that I wrote when I was high. I say I'm a queen when I write drunk because I drink the finest quality nectar. It's always connected. If I write a paragraph while drinking Pabst, you can smell it and taste it in the text. It's cheap shit. You put that in your novel to add length, to flesh out, prepare a more important paragraph. That's how novels work. It's like Tetris but with paragraphs.

I'm fasting. I fast all the time. My mind alert all the time. Always good and sensible. Taking my medications at the right time. Always timed. For the rest of my life. That's not nothing. It might be ten years, the rest of my life. It might be just five. I would be pretty sad to find out that I only had a few months left after spending these few days doing nothing. That's why I always have to write everything down. Just in case.

My stepmother, Catherine, met the police officers who "found" Guy Turcotte's children. She served them in her restaurant all the time. They'd burned out, both of them.

A scene that marks you, that makes you want to move to a country without children, no children, ever. I saw Innocence on a list of ridiculous baby names of 2013 on the Internet recently. Innocence Turcotte. There was also Marie-Mercredi and Cash. When you name your children after payday, you know you have a serious problem. Cash Monique. The Trois-Rivières Pussy Festival. Wordplay, information, I've got all that. I`m really good at titles. My uncle says I should sell them. My uncle is a capitalist. Like everyone. He doesn't understand what I write. Titles are short, efficient. You can make a list of them. Browse literature. Upload it, stream it. Window-shop forever. Reread everything, into life everlasting. Hashtag poetry. Geneviève Desrosiers fell off a balcony during a party. They don't know if she jumped or just fell. Kate Middleton's nurse committed suicide. I can't stop thinking about famous deaths. Ève Cournoyer committed suicide on August 12, 2012.

Why, Ève?
I didn't know you.
I can only imagine.
I'll make you a modern Marie-Soleil.
Why, Ève?
You had a choice.
I kind of understand.
I've had the thoughts that precede the action.
I'd take blue pills.
The whole bottle.

I'm back home. My grandmother came for dinner. My

uncle brought her. My grandmother has a dropped cerebellum. She was born like that. Nothing can be done. The doctors can't operate. Like me. She's losing all her senses. Now she can only see glimmers, and you have to put yourself right in her field of vision, so she can associate a voice with a face, so she can follow the conversation and understand when we're speaking to her. She's been in a wheelchair since she was young. Before that, it was a walker. My mother and my uncle have taken care of their mother their whole lives. My grandfather was an alcoholic. Difficult lives. I was happy to go to my half-sister's in Saint-Agathe and give my mother a break. I'm going to end up like my grandmother if my tumour comes back. My tumour is right in the control centre of my body. I'll have to kill myself if I want to avoid being like my grandmother. I half think about it. I don't want to think about it. I can say anything because you're never sure if I'm joking or if I'm serious. If it's fiction or if it's not. I light the two candles. I tell you to stare into the flames. You start seeing double. Drama queens.

My mother just texted me from my room.
"The little girl upstairs is playing in her room,
    right above yours."
I'm here taking a shit in the bathroom.
Do you feel me?
Do you smell the odour of the cigarette smoke mixing
    with the odour of shit?
I'll give you a few clues.
How my apartment is arranged.
I make a little path with bread crumbs,

from my bedroom to the bathroom.
I hope you're hungry.
That you feel like a bird.
Move the book away from your face.
The book stinks.
I'm making a fool of you.
Toss me aside.
Put down the book.
Go on, put it down.
Give me your most disapproving look.
I understand.

Is that better? I promise I won't do it anymore. It made me feel better to think on the floor in my corner. About our relationship. Don't you think we're beautiful together? We have a wonderful love/hate relationship. A prime example. If I spoke through a cupcake, would that be better? You'll be a chocolate éclair and I'll be a cupcake. I'm nice. I'm casting you in a good part. An éclair is quick and everyone loves chocolate. Except my stepfather, who's allergic. But I'm not writing this book for him. I'm writing it for you. You bought it with your own money. I belong to you. My whole life in your hands. Your hands. Your breasts make me want to eat pizza pockets. Raphaël, your penis makes me want to eat a pear. You have fucking huge balls. It's a sight. Maman, I love you. Papa, I'm sorry for always talking about your testicles. Reader, you're a cupcake. I hope everyone's happy.

Steak

A VICTORIA LOVE FILM

When I got back, my friends were awake.
We went out for breakfast. I was expecting a
restaurant that served steak. Everything is better
with a steak. From breakfast to dinner.
Steak on the side. Salad, rice are more of a bed.
I'd take a nap on it. I'd take a nap on anything and
I'd eat all the time. That's what the cortisone does.
I annoyed everyone with my zoo photos on Facebook
for twenty-four hours. I don't know how to
make an album. I don't know how to make
a film, or how to describe one. I know how
to be inspired and that's more than enough.

THE END

PART TWO

VICTORIA LOVE

The book is in the film, the film is in the book. The lover is in the tree. The theatre is full of pears. I could carry on with the songs, to get to know them and everything. The pineapple is growing and I look at it. Better. I throw it into strawberry Jell-O with diving goggles. I have a video of it. God, that was a beautiful day.

MAGGIE BOOKS

All this may be full of the beautiful achievement that is life but it makes me want to vomit. I scratch imaginary sores on my neck. I create employment for my hand. I drink coffee. I prefer to imagine that it comes straight from the machine, and that the roast is the name of a dead plant. Like Latin, a dead language that is now a dance, all in the hips. When Marie-Antoinette tries to dance to anything with a Latin rhythm, Benjamin says she looks like a wriggling fish. I say: like a burning flame. I say: like molten lava. I say that nature is cruel too, and that everyone forgets that. I'm going to cloister myself in concrete macramé. A labyrinth. This is all the fault of the fucking hippies, and Benjamin has a beard and hair that are straight-up smokable. That creates employment for his lungs. And for Marie-Antoinette's lungs too. I'm going to jerk off comfortably, thinking of her in a flowered dress, giggling and shaking her hips in a field of strawberries and innocence. That's all Marie-Antoinette eats—cocks. Why doesn't she eat mine? I'm going to think about Nyan Cat and Pikachu, about student videos with way too many special effects. I wonder who Nyan Cat and Pikachu would pick for a threesome. Everything has to be sexual in my brain. The lobes spread open and my tears lubricate. I'm in love with a fucking hippie. That's my fucking drama. It's not my fucking business what Nyan Cat and Pikachu do with their free time. My father definitely taught me not to swear, but I don't remember. Fucking huge explosion. Way too many special effects. In *(III)* by Crystal Castles, it's like there's a squirrel playing the xylophone, that's enough for me. If I can't remember what a squirrel looks like, I go on Wikipedia. I chill out in Google Images or go to Parc La Fontaine on Google Street View. Benjamin is going to have children with Marie-Antoinette. I'm going to keep stalking her. Even when she has a big pregnant belly. Because I love her. Marie-Antoinette will roll up her cheeks, Benjamin will smoke them, and I'll film the two of them, record it all. I'll make animated GIFs of their lovemaking. I'll Auto-Tune their moaning and laugh. Abs of steel in my concrete building. My search history is going to be super explicit. Cunt, pussy, corn on the cob, tits, fennec, Marie-Antoinette happy, Benjamin faithful. Skyblog reality. I'm going to talk about them on the Internet. The Internet is my buddy. My only friend. I'm going to feel two paws gripping my right thigh, my hair is going to stand on end with the static. I'll see a little gleam of yellow looming in the darkness. My iTunes will play the Crystal Castles album on repeat. My speakers will undulate. Listen, little poodle. The tiny paws pull down my G-string. Sex poodle. Fuck everything, fuck aspirations. I'm throwing myself into video. I'm filming everything.

Rapunzel

In a room: a dancer.

Legos to represent her hair.

Tiny spoons for her teeth.

Coconuts for her pendulous breasts.

Two pool balls for her eyes.

Her body outlined in wire covered in candy, chocolate, jelly beans, licorice.

A bathing suit patchworked with the logos of popular brands, Baby Phat, Rocawear, Miss Sixty...

A pole made of a long, thin fork. The teeth of the fork are covered in little mirrored squares like a disco ball, to show that it's for eating luxury and caviar.

Once upon a time there was a girl with long hair. It was me. Ariel was chilling in my ears. Be careful what you say. In general. But especially you, Ariel. In the real story, you end up as sea foam and you sing like a nightingale that chain-smoked its whole life.

I'm lucky to have a big ass. It's like a built-in cushion for couches and chairs. Human cushions. Mélissa says a big ass like mine is mostly made of mayonnaise. She's as flat as a board but all the women in her family needed breast reductions.

I wonder if Beyoncé reads Asimov. I wonder if cheerleaders read Asimov. I don't dare read him because I'm not pretty anymore. I wonder if Scarlett Johansson reads Asimov, if Mahée Paiement does.

I need to take advantage of this time. I don't know why,

but when I woke up from my afternoon nap, I couldn't feel the water in my ear anymore. I need to hurry. Pretty soon, I'll drop something. I'll bend over and the water will resurface. It's definitely down there, the asshole. I don't come up with possible scenarios. I know it's there somewhere. I have to pay attention to my head. I hold it up straight. I don't look too bright with my Jell-O-legged walk and my head on pause. Pretty soon, I won't be able to write anymore. Don't tell that to my new boss. Don't tell that to my publisher. I said ten years, ten books. Big liar.

I got accosted by some girl out in front of Le Square, a restaurant trying hard to be chic on Prince Arthur. French. I hate the French. I hate the Québécois too. I hate everyone. I would have stayed home hiding out in my apartment, but it was Mathieu's birthday. I was thinking about that WD-40 tune about the girl from Amos. *J'pense à toi quand j'me crosse.* That there is poetry. Everything else is just fucking around. People who abuse the Enter and Tab keys. Too breathless to speak. I'm going to write poetry at the end of my life. When I have to sell my book I often say: the sentences are short. I don't explain that I have to type with one hand, that each sentence is a struggle. That would be too heavy. The girl wanted a cigarette. I was on the phone with Mathieu. She didn't care. She went to dig into my purse. I put my call on hold. I gave her a cigarette and a light. I told her she had no class. She didn't give a shit. She was looking at my bag, salivating. Ah. There's nothing in there. The loot is in my head. In my sick head.

A little girl cries at the foot of a tree.
Her cat is caught on a branch.
A cat cries at the foot of a tree.
Its little girl is caught on a branch.

Nothing works anymore. I'm writing in a black document, because I'm in a black mood. The black document doesn't tell me when I make mistakes. The white document is a fucking cunt for that. I'm slowly recovering from my disease, they never stop changing my medications, I am a big Shuffle button, now more than ever. The white document is blank. I write little paragraphs in green on a black background. Little bits of daily life. Breath and aspirations. Green wind on black background. I tell myself it's better to be interesting for the whole world, with the torments of my daily life, because that's all I manage to write. My daily life. Mine. Not that of a character.

Black document. Dark goddess reporting. If only e-books came in white on a black background. I'd read a little then. I'd do my intellectual duty. But no. What am I doing? What's new? They ask me constantly. News. Stuff. I do nothing. I watch TV. I eat ice cream. I don't even save my documents. I go into the black one and I write my notes from the day. It doesn't give meaning to my days. Writing is not the key. You have to live too. I said so many times, when everyone thought I was at death's door, that being depressed is for living people. Suddenly they give me a few more years to live and what's the first thing I do with this precious time? I get depressed. I take pills on a fixed schedule and I am depressed. I have a hole in my head and it depresses me.

Black document. The goddess still just as dark. The paragraphs still just as small. There's not much to do in my château. I'm like Rapunzel in her tower. Kill some princesses, that's what I'll do. I came home in a taxi from a family dinner at Au Petit Extra with that idea in mind. I'll kill princesses. I'll be a princess-serial-killer-slash-writer. They'll put that beneath my name. Known for.

Rapunzel is a temperamental princess. She shuts herself up in her tower, roams around with her hand to her forehead. Her friends wait for her at the foot of the tower. They ring. They get the fuck out of there. Nobody ever goes in. She doesn't answer the door. She plays dead. She holds the curtains so they won't move. She's not there. Leave your packages by the door. Her friends wait for a bit but they get sick of waiting. Which is fine. The curtains are starting to mess up her cuticles. She's not equipped for socializing. She has that long hair that makes her look ugly. She looks like an old hippie, she doesn't want her friends to see her like this. She wants to remain the beautiful postcard queen. The beautiful, strong, serene girl of their memories. She doesn't want them to see her like this, all shabby in her old dress. The dress used to be dazzling. Now it's been through some shit, it's seen other dresses.

I understand why serial killers kill their victims in their basement or their barn. They need to concentrate. Because sometimes serial killers have families. A wife, children, an above-ground pool. They have to bring people underground at all costs, it's psychological. I wonder if the family, the wife especially, suspects anything about the father's activities. I wonder why serial killers are always men. I wonder if my mother suspects. If she knows I'm killing princesses in my room.

I have no basement. I'll never find a publisher.

They found Rapunzel's body in a pool of blood. The circumstances of her death are unknown. This was not a good idea. I opened my white document, I wrote Rapunzel's name, I made her speak. Not a good idea. Stay in the black document.

I was watching Canal D. It took two years for them to find Sister Estelle's murderer. The dude ended up getting acquitted too. Because he was epileptic and bipolar. The dude killed a nun. If you can believe that. A nice, helpful nun. He was acquitted for ridiculous reasons. What am I doing? Making myself afraid of everyone?

Shawn is epileptic. Daniel is bipolar. Tomorrow, Shawn is going to be awarded a trophy designed by me. While that's happening, Daniel will be taking care of me. Someone has to take care of me. I can't stay alone too long.

Tomorrow they will get all dressed up.
The poets, the cartoonists, the literature students,

everyone, they'll go to the Gala of the Academy of
Literary Life at the Turn of the XXI Century.
I'll stay shut up in my tower.
I can't climb the stairs anymore.
It's depressing, but it's not dying that depresses me.
It's the void.
It's everywhere around me.
My head is empty.
A cavity, I wish.
A big dirty hole would be no worse.
I won't have time to speak or organize.
I feel sick.
I have to talk about it.
I'm alone and empty.

My feet hurt this morning. It's like I climbed Kilimanjaro in
my sleep. My legs are finished. I need new ones. I massage
them, crying. It hurts a lot. I do a fucking ton of hiking in
my sleep. I did the Camino de Santiago, and right now I'm
on top of the highest mountain in the world. The plane
ticket didn't cost much. My pussy smells like pussy. At least
that's consistent. Smells are important.

I wake up again with bad pains in my legs. At ten minutes
to two in the morning. They're not used to it. Pills in Jell-O,
I feel them this morning. I stagger and weave, and not for
any fun reason. It hurts. It really fucking hurts. I ask a lot of
my body these days. I hope this isn't a permanent situation.
Not the collapse already. I'm a soldier, I can take more. It
still makes me laugh a little that everything is such a process.

The "breakfast" process is the hardest. I knock into myself with the walker. I've slept badly, I have to brush my teeth in the kitchen sink with my shaking legs. The bathroom sink is blocked. I don't need obstacles. My apartment is already enough of an obstacle course as it is. I'm going to have to be served breakfast in bed like a princess. Never mind. It went fine in the end. Didn't have to call my mother.

I wake up in the middle of the night. My legs are totally useless. I have to hold on to the counter to walk. In the darkness. I grab on to the table and it tips over. I'm afraid to make myself a bowl of cereal. The last time, I dropped it on my foot. My big toe was swollen. It's the extremity of one of my legs. Getting back to my room was even harder. I'm not lame enough already, universe? Sometimes I think the universe is checking me out with its X-ray glasses and having a good laugh. The universe does not have enough fennec foxes.

The palliative care lady came over to my house. People are going to come see me at home now. To "care for" me. She suggested a commode and diapers. It's already pretty depressing to have to use a walker at twenty-three years old, to have to wait for my mother to take a bath. I'd like it if my mother were made of metal and if she finished work earlier. As it is now, we have two hours together. I eat, she helps me bathe, and it's already bedtime.

Buffalo '89

A VINCENT GALLO FILM

Waiting for the bus means checking if it's coming.
A glance to the left here and there. It works out well
that the left side of my vision is a dead zone.
I'm badly designed for a sick person. The "taking the
bus" process takes a long time to get going. I have
to get up from my seat. I'm going to
Marie-Antoinette's. I'm getting out of prison.
Killed too many princesses. I'm going to steal a car. I
saw a guy do it on TV. Something about licorice. Or
cheese twists. A Tex-Mex thread. We're going to
drink this bottle of '89 port our father
gave me when I got out of prison.

THE END

Marie-Antoinette Love

You enter a large room. A giant transparent bowl. Inside, human beings of different sizes, naked, floating like peas. Yellow liquid. For spices, the fifty or so American stars. For more seasoning, shreds of American flags.

A big yellow spoon with a smiley face on the bowl. You stand just beneath it. You feel so small. You smile back at it.

The handle is made of yellow logs attached to one another, covered in plastic flowers, also yellow, and poppies, to represent the fantasies engraved on the stylish, beautiful cutlery.

Marie-Antoinette, filmed by her new friend Maggie Books, making a starfish shape in a bowl. The star on the Sunday. The day of the Sun, the day of the Lord, the day of the worst of all the colours.

Marie-Antoinette, my beloved sister, I'm thinking of you this morning. A pizza pocket. The bit of pasta leftover from yesterday, brought back from Grandma's. Noon: use of the microwave. It was you, my beautiful sister of love, who loaned it to me. I'm thinking of you, sister. I still have the reflex to call her "little sister." She's taller than me. All the updates to be carried out. I don't call her by her name. Even if a name is all we have in this lowly world.

Jérôme Gendreau	Spoiled brat number one
Audrey-Anne Gendreau	Spoiled brat number two
Pierrette Gendreau	The grandma who serves Bottero wine
Esteban Gendreau	The uncle who watched too many New Age documentaries
Maxime Gendreau	The firefighter uncle with a taste for arson

Alain Gendreau	The father with stretch-marked testicles
Marie-Antoinette Love	Queen of fuck-all
Victoria Love	Drama queen

No. It wasn't squash on the menu yesterday at Grandma Pierrette's. I thought it'd be best to make it funny and to write you. When I came home yesterday, I just felt like bawling. I'd thought to myself: *Never again.* I really should have listened to myself. We have just one life to live and I will not be spending any more of mine with those people. Maybe it's cold and shameless, but that's how I feel, so what can I do? It's stronger than me. I'd like to have another last name. Before, my initials bugged me because I thought they were tacky. Now it's reached a whole new level. My name is Victoria Love Gendreau. I'd rather be named Victoria Love Chouinard, even if Chouinard makes me think of Swiss chard and that's my least favourite food. Really another level. I'll keep the Gendreau, because I already published a book with that name and changing it is expensive. They don't even realize that it's cool that our name is part of literature, thanks to me. Nobody understood my book. I'm fairly certain that nobody except Papa read it. But everyone talked to me about it. Like it was some ordinary thing. With all the usual stupid questions. "Are you still writing? Are you working on another book?" You don't really want me to answer. You're not really interested. You ask me that to fill the silence. Because it's awkward. Everything's awkward when you start the conversation with boring questions. It's a bad start. We'll sit in silence and stare at the fire. No, the

TV. We'll turn on the TV and watch it together as a family. I like watching TV with my mother in our pyjamas and everything. But come on, it's Christmas. Can I go one night of the year without having to watch Véronique Cloutier host something?

So there it is, the setup. Well, Marie-Antoinette, you're definitely pretty lucky to not have to go to the hospital too often. The lighting, my god. The lighting is like a hospital cafeteria. Or Giant Tiger. Full neon. And the dimmer in the kitchen is broken. So forget dimming the lights. Hello, Tylenol. I felt like I was in a bad dream, or a bad movie. Grandma had bought everything pre-made.

The first thing I did when I got there was open a beer. I figured I shouldn't get too drunk. I say whatever comes into my head lately. I have no filter. Literature thinks that's just fine. Family would like it if you were a little less pathetic, a little more like the others. Competitive figure skating. So yeah, I opened the fridge. You learn a lot about people by looking at the contents of their fridge. Just pre-prepared stuff. There were a bunch of empty boxes on a counter. Tourtières, packets of sauce, you name it. She has no problem advertising the fact that she doesn't put in any effort. The lighting would have been less terrible if she'd had those spiral energy-saving bulbs. I would have thought: *Aw, cute, Grandma cares about the environment.* But no. She just bought the cheapest bulbs. And she's not ashamed of showing it. With her broken dimmer. Too cheap to pay for an electrician. Too cheap to repair her pipes. She talked about it, oh yes. In the ocean of conversation topics, choose the one you know the best: being cheap. Apparently the pipes are a bit blocked. The downstairs neighbour, the nice white man, he's waiting for Grandma to get her pipes fixed because he's got water coming up through his tub. I felt like knocking on his door. "Just move, man. She's never going to fix those pipes."

We can smoke in the garage. I smoked so many cigarettes, just to escape. To pass the time, I guess. I'm coughing like an old man this morning. It's not sexy. I wasn't far from the neighbour. I couldn't stop thinking about him. I was thinking how someone has to save him, someone has to tell him he's living beneath a fucking crazy woman, that his pipes were going to keep backing up, that the smell of rotten eggs in the bathroom is permanent, it's included in the rent. Your apartment is far away from everything and it smells like shit. Your apartment includes a fireplace you can't use, and the landlord's son is a fucking firefighter, so that's how cheap she is.

Maxime's new girlfriend is named Nadine. She's really nice. A super-normal girl. I'm happy to have met her. Chain-smoking with someone else is not as bad. You feel like it's less bad for your lungs. There'll be four raspy lungs tomorrow morning rather than two. I am not alone. But fuck, I felt alone. Nadine was upstairs. I went down with my phone to call my mother. I needed to talk to someone. I wanted to call you, Marie-Antoinette Love, but I wouldn't have known where to begin. Everything about that dinner was upsetting.

First: I couldn't invite my mother. Because my father didn't want her there. It didn't fit with his little vision of the evening. Wake up. We're not a perfect family. We really aren't. Call your daughter. Make an effort. I'd come back to another supper like this if you made an effort, but for now I'm clocking out. I went downstairs. Smoked another cigarette. Without Nadine. Then I called my mother because I felt like bawling. I keep wondering: *What am I doing here?* And there's no magic answer. There's no magic in life. The world is cruel. I live in reality. Not in an illusion. I started wanting to bawl because of our uncle Esteban. He started telling me how I could heal with positive thinking. Alright, you. Jesus Christ. There's a whole TEAM of DOCTORS (you know, like, people who went to school for a long time) who told me that I'm NOT going to get better, that THIS is what's going to fucking kill me, and you, you're making me explain this to you out loud at my first family dinner in years because you read one and a half paragraphs somewhere on what Véronique Cloutier has to say on positive thinking. What? Should I congratulate you for having read the full one and a half paragraphs?

It's like Grandma. She told me she read my book three times. Then she looked at me with her fish eyes. I, like, understood that to mean it was my turn to speak. So I said: "Ah." What do you say to that? It's like when you recognize someone in the street but you don't say hi; you don't cross the street to interrupt them listening to their iPod, you just note it in your head. You think: *There's Untel. I don't want to talk to him. I'm going to stay on my side of the street.* If you mention it to Untel the next time you see him, you can't be surprised if he says, "Ah." It's so empty. There's an echo in the void. There's a big fucking echo in Grandma's head. She could read my book forty times and she wouldn't understand it any better. Even if it was pre-prepared, the way she likes it. Even if I wasn't reinventing the wheel. Not because she's stupid. No. Just because she can't manage to get out of her own life, her own little existence, to dive into someone else's. These people don't understand love. These people don't live. These people buy pre-made tourtière and give money in red envelopes. These people arrange the envelopes under a little fibre-optic Christmas tree from Walmart. Full of mistakes: "Mery Cristmas and Happy new Year's." Understanding nothing. Asking stupid questions. Talking bullshit.

I miss you so much! I thought about you so much yesterday. I really wanted to text you. But to say what? Thirty-six thousand things you already know? We have a shit family. We live in a cruel world. Bah. Merry Christmas and Happy New Year. If you ask me, we're much better off without them. I know it's cold to say that. My mother argues with me and tells me to let them in. They just have to read my books to find out what's going on with me. That's my logic. It's cold, yes, but it's winter, so fuck it.

So yeah. Hospital lighting, dry turkey (the only thing she cooked), ketchup from the drugstore, the litre of Bottero on the table, the pitiful little tree in the living room, the TV on: not a beautiful slice of life to report to my friends. Nothing to say. Nothing to add.

"What did you do over the holidays?"

"Not much. Partied."

I didn't touch the bottle of Bottero. I drank my father's fancy wine. Portuguese. Jérôme wanted to impress everyone with his Spanish. I only took one year of Spanish but I knew he was making mistakes. He was sitting at the kitchen counter with his sister. They still put the children at the counter. It's depressing. I think I was supposed to take the third spot. But I didn't want to sit in the corner. I'm twenty-tree. That's five more than eighteen. I sat at the table and I drank red wine. So there. Grandma took the third spot at the counter. She sat down saying she doesn't see her grandchildren very often. That made it seem like she was going to talk to them. But she spent the whole meal turned toward us. Because yes, youth is boring. Audrey-Anne and Jérôme are nothing without Facebook. They spent their evening in the office. On the Internet, together. A lovely activity. So yes, Grandma doesn't connect well with the young people. They're not interested in her pipes. They don't remember the woman upstairs like she does. She can't talk to them about her.

I'm not kidding. I'm not kidding when I say that Jérôme brought his red envelope to the table and later said he'd opened it in the living room before to see. Audrey-Anne made a fan with the money she received and started fanning her face with her Christmas loot, looking at her brother. I'm not kidding. This really happened. In our faces and everything. Everyone laughed. Ha ha ha, the children got money. Ha ha ha, Audrey-Anne's fanning herself with our bills. Ho ho ho. I'm the only one who brought a wrapped present. And it was bigger than the tree. Grandma explained why she doesn't do gifts anymore: "We need money," "We know better what we want." (No more birdfeeders, Marie-Antoinette Love! Are you sad?) Ask me questions, I'll answer. My mother said I have to let them in, I'd love to answer questions, play the game.

Jesus. I started writing to you two hours ago. I'm up to three pages. I got carried away. And I still have a ton of things to say. I feel dirty. Everyone noticed that my face is swollen. Everyone can see it easily, that I look like I'm pregnant with the baby Jesus because of my water retention. I had a family dinner at my other uncle's the day before and, in comparison, let's say I have a favourite family. We made jokes. We talked about other things. It distracted me. I don't have to be sick all the time. I can forget about it with them. I smoke way fewer cigarettes when I think about that. About them. I don't get pissed off about boring questions. I find them cute. I answer. We make more jokes. My uncle gave me a Magic Bullet Deluxe. I kept telling my mother that I wanted a blender. The stars love me. I still haven't had breakfast. I'm going to make myself something with my new machine. I'll post photos of smoothies and milkshakes on Facebook for weeks, months. I'm going to gain even more weight, because I'm going to eat even more ice cream. Two baby Jesuses. Three. Thirty-six thousand. Way past December.

It really messed me up spending the evening at Pierrette's. With Papa. As his daughter, the author. Even if I'm the same daughter, the same author who just published her very first book, rich with her first cancer, young, and the first star of the family, the first one to be on TV. I'm the same daughter everywhere. But I feel uneasy in my body when I'm with Papa's family. I would have liked to vomit somewhere. And not tell Grandma. So she'd step in it. In the dark night. Not red like the envelopes, not red like Christmas. Merry Christmas and Happy New Year. I love you in every fucking colour. I'm proud to be a member of your family. For me, the Gendreaus are you and me, Marie-Antoinette Love. That's more than enough and it's just fine like that. I can't wait to see you and I think of you often.

Poetry and Cigarettes
A JIM JARMUSCH FILM
The girl clearly slept with the publisher.
The book really pissed me off. It starts by
talking about true death. I get up in the night.
I make myself a bowl of cereal in the
dark. I dreamed I was a contestant on
Come Dine with Me. I'd gotten to the dessert part,
so I woke up. Two thirty. Fuck. I was making
chocolate ice cream. My cereal seems boring.
I made a top-quality turd. I didn't see it.
Darkness required. But the texture was right.
Poetry and shit, it's the same colour.
THE END

Snow White

We convinced famous people to draw an L on their foreheads to say they've also failed at times. An L for Love, not for Loser. A beautiful L, with beautiful lipstick. On the video, we see them making faces, with different hairstyles, different hair colours.

Right in the middle of the room where the video is projected, a Rubik's Cube made of traffic lights. We're going in so many directions. You don't mind. Your legs can handle it.

Once upon a time, that time passed quickly and there were seven little people. Simone de Beauvoir wasn't pressed for time. She had time for a cup of tea before writing. Sometimes she went shopping too. She'd spend time with her friends in the afternoon. She'd read the newspaper. I'm a little jealous. I'm so pressed for time that everything I say has to be literary. Genet wrote in huge chunks. Twelve hours a day for six months. I'm more of a prison than a country garden. Too bad. Flowers are so beautiful. We'd have to be able to smoke in prison. I'd be going. For having killed those princesses, of course.

I invited my friends who've been taking care of me to Nil Bleu, an Ethiopian restaurant. It's the perfect type of cuisine for me. You eat everything with your fingers. I looked up the menu on the Internet beforehand. There were blue drinks. The drinks weren't exactly blue when they arrived at the table. I was a little disappointed. I couldn't drink until very recently. If I'm promised blue, I want blue. In any case, it didn't make me regret leaving Facebook for two seconds. I miss playing Scrabble with Aimée Verret. Even if I lost all the time. My face is pulsating. I know what that word means. Doesn't get you a lot of points, but it's pretty. Everyone sent me nice encouraging messages. It's distracting in the long run. And drunk people on Facebook do sketchy things. I wake up when the bars are closing. It turns the world upside down for these people to see me online. The indecent proposals make me laugh. You apparently haven't heard yet, and haven't seen me in a long time. Yeah, I'll jump in a taxi. I hope you have a lot of lube and a fucking good sense of humour. I want a blue drink and a lot of honey.

I gave gifts to my friends. I wonder if Simone went shopping for gifts too, if Genet had an eBay account and computer access. There was this girl selling her virginity on eBay. What a princess.

I'm the cousin of a figure skater but I'm no beauty on the ice. Winter is not my friend. I fall into every snowbank. They're so big and high that no one really notices. It sucks being sick in winter.

Every morning, I wake up and thank the stars. My fear is to never wake up again. Sudden death. Anyone can die in their sleep. It's just more likely it'll be me. I have the hiccups this morning. I throw up in my mouth and swallow it back down. No waste.

In fifteen minutes, I'm going to have my first enema. I have fifteen minutes to take my clothes off and get in the bath. I was sitting there comfortably, looking up stuff on Wikipedia. It's part of my routine. There are no tips for preparing for enemas in the entry for sapphism. I type with one hand. My father has started typing with one finger. My mother is going to put this plastic finger in my ass. My asshole more red than pink. She'll inject the liquid. I'll take a shit. That's the concept. All I'm good for is learning. And bending over to receive. Or to vacate.

OK. "Breakfast" process. It's five forty-six in the morning. Let's see how long this takes me. OK. It's six ten. Time stresses me out a little. A little: I almost find that funny. It's not so bad. I throw up in my mouth again a little and I swallow. Nothing wants to stay inside my body. I drool on my cigarettes. The filters are all soaked. Tomorrow, a volunteer is coming to take care of me. That makes me nervous. She's going to see me eat. I don't feel like putting on a show.

Waking up in the middle of the night makes me want to listen to Leonard Cohen. It's seven minutes past midnight. I slept about four hours already. That's not enough. Time counts double. I do a bunch of things at once. It would be cool if I could do the same thing while sleeping. Not depressing sick-person things like pissing. I don't want to regress. I already talk about my shit enough.

I slept another three and a half hours. My nights are fragmented. I wake up to write a few words. In the dark. Mathieu would freak out. He has a phobia of sticky things. I'm full of honey. My keyboard is dripping.

The dripping makes me think of the night Jacinthe was totally loaded at Showgirl, the bar in Laval where I was making my debut. Ben had wanted to celebrate it, he'd bought a cake. Bad idea. Jacinthe danced in it, got it everywhere. Mathieu would have left the bar. The second time I saw her, she was at Carol in Quebec City and she seemed totally normal. Jacinthe is like the name of a white girl who tries to talk like she's black. She was talking with the other girls. But she said nothing about the cake night. I should say that, at Showgirl, she'd stolen one girl's makeup kit and a hundred American dollars from my wallet I'd left on the edge of the stage, a new girl move. Not the kind of night she'd want to brag about.

There are so many things to do, so many things to say. I should have taken notes, made a glossary, indexed and organized the entries. Now it's too late. My past has long since passed. I have to get swept up in nostalgia to write. To remember the good old times.

I have to live in the past. The life of a sick girl isn't interesting to you. It's OK. Big head, big memory. Twenty-three years and now to live for two, maybe three. Full box. Pow.

That night, I woke up at two in the morning. Total darkness. I like snacking in total darkness. With just the light of my computer. I feel sheltered. That night everything went really badly. I started by making myself a bowl of cereal. But there was no more milk. I wanted to make toast with peanut butter and raspberry jam. I dropped the plate on the big toe of my right foot. I fell down. In pain. I cried. I swore. I left it all there. The bowl, the cereal, the condiments, the plate on the ground, the bread in the toaster. I just took a pink pill to calm my head. The top of my Yop bottle got lost in my books. Nothing was going right that night. Jell-O legs. Legs are fucking useful. I thought I was going to feel the damage to my right foot when I woke up. I don't feel very much of what happens anymore. My whole right side. It's starting again. It hurts to say it out loud. Yesterday my mother wanted to kick my ass. Because I hadn't done anything all day. It hurts to say it out loud: I can't concentrate anymore, the letters in the books are too small, the new chemo is more brutal than the last round, it takes everything out of me. The old chemo isn't working anymore, I'm going to die. It's closing in so fast.

I have to go to bed. Pills. Kisses. I scored a new sleeping pill. I'm a bit sad because of my Jell-O legs. It means I can't sleep at Mathieu's anymore. He has a loft bed. Have you ever tried to climb down a ladder with Jell-O legs?

My legs still hurt. My knees especially. I put on a necklace. I already have a necklace of swollen lymph nodes. I add another. I need to look cute, my mother's friends are coming over this morning. I wear dresses now. They're less complicated to put on. I don't know what to expect. Every day is a gamble. I feel super good this morning. I'm writing with one hand. I'm seeing double. It's all relative. My right foot is seriously swollen. But I feel super good, for real. If having a swollen foot makes me a contemporary Cinderella, my Prince Charming is going to be looking for me for a long time. Especially since I'm off Facebook now. I'm going to retain water in my right foot. I'm going to have new stretch marks. I'd like to have one in the shape of a C for Cinderella. Built-in. Pretty please.

Insect

(Based on *Incest* by Christine Angot)
DJ Wildchild. Super-early super-intense sets. *Ting*.
Turn all the pages. Read with one distracted eye.
Everything that's happening in the world,
everything that's happening to you. From the
corner of your eye. The bedbug dances
to the rhythm of the jukebox.
They only want you when you're seventeen.
When you're twenty-one, you're no fun.

THE END

Alice in Chains

In a fairly big room, a white rabbit in a tutu. Held on a metal leash by a blasé Maggie. She films the rabbit with her other hand. She looks around, sighing. You don't want to be her friend.

I get hostile when I haven't eaten. On my mug, Garfield thinks: *I'm easy to get along with when things go my way.* He thinks that in a cloud. But I don't like clouds. It would be better if he said it aloud. Anyway. My mother just lectured me because I smoke too many cigarettes. I'm coughing a little, it's difficult to speak this morning. She's right. But it's the only little pleasure I have left.

"Maman, stop lecturing me."

Alice. That's what we named our white rabbit, Francis, Isabelle, and I. It's also my mother's name. In chains. Like the band. My main nurse. Somewhere in a closet, she has a little costume like they sell at Halloween. Gifts for my nurse friends. I gave Mathieu a belt made from a seat belt from a car. For Britney, a shirt with two skulls and a pink lemur giving kisses. For Alice, my mother, a black watch with leather loops. That's kind of a gift for me. I'm constantly asking her the time. Dying is stressful.

"Maman, what time is it? Mathieu isn't here."

It's three in the morning. I'm a bit pissed off. Everything is set up in the apartment so that my mornings go smoothly. I went to bed at eight thirty. I woke up around midnight, blue pill. And then, oh hey, awake at three in the morning. If I can manage a nap before taking my cortisone (around six), excellent. But I'll wake up my mother. Coffee, pills, breakfast. I'll manage it. I massage my legs. I put on a robe when I got up so as not to traumatize you.

"Maman, can you get some things for tomorrow morning and put them in my room: a blue pill, a little bit of Ensure, a maple butter sandwich for my midnight snack?"

Every day is my birthday. I ordered myself a birthday cake for tonight. It's April 4. I'm indulging myself a little. The fourteenth is not far off. I'm not going to make it till then. I'll be twenty-three forever. We'll see. Tonight I want to eat my cake with my hands. Like at the Ethiopian restaurant. I want to have cake everywhere, like in baby pictures. Yesterday I fell asleep in the candy bowl. Let's think about nice things. Like my birthday.

"Maman, I want jewellery and a little dress for Sunday. And for right now, pear and cranberry black tea."

I'm trying hard to change my schedule. I really make a big effort. It's exhausting. I just woke up my mother for the first time. For my morning pills, my juice, and to warn her that she'll be woken up around six. In the meantime, I'll play with the cereal Sam brought me. And read poems. As if I was eating them. It's a bit like that for me with poetry. A treat. Love is on the island. Lust is in the syrup and the syrup is on the snow. Sex is a deserted beach named desire.

"Maman, can you cut up some strawberries before you go shopping?"

I ate big American strawberries. Full of GMOs. Crates of strawberries. Without the whipped cream and the suave look that go with them. Now I regret it. It would have made for a nice scene to describe. More important, it would have been something different, given you a break from me whining about my new body. I played *suave* in my Scrabble game with Sam. Yes, Sam the guy who didn't want me in my first book. We played in French even though we were both talking about our trips to the States. In French, not like with Aimée Verret on Facebook. I didn't put the word *kiwi*, for forty-four points. I didn't put *zizi*, Britney Speaks's last name. We had so many things to say, Sam and me. I put *suave* and then we put away the game, it was time to eat. I was wearing my beautiful outfit, a feather necklace, my tiara. We ordered sushi. I was a bit afraid he'd die. We'd forgotten to ask them to skip the shrimp. He's allergic.

"Maman, can you bring me pillows so I can put up my foot? And Tylenol? And some Ensure? And some things to eat so I can take care of my baby Jesus?"

My back hurts. I have to put my foot up in the air today. Yesterday it was on the ground almost all day. It's bigger and more swollen. I'll have to spend most of my day with my foot higher than my heart. What's a day? It's being afraid of dying at any minute. Of going out in convulsions.

"Maman, I need help. I just fell down."

You should see the big bruise I have on my right hip. It's traumatizing. I fell down. It's a lot of weight on my hip. My mother said it'll turn yellow. The colour of bananas, urine, egg yolks. Sunshine too. Lucky thing we have corn there to save the whole world. Don't worry, I won't put that in my ass. My mother can't stand the smell of bananas. She buys them for me anyway. I have to hide them in my bedroom. Bananas are difficult to manage. Mango is more friendly. It takes its time going bad. I make smoothies every morning. Banana, mango, field berries. Nobody would dare tell me I'm out in left field. The poor little sick girl.

"Maman, can you make me a smoothie this morning?"

I promise I won't put any more bananas in my texts. I want my mother to be able to read my book. A banana is the opposite of timeless. What would I seem like if, three days after you bought my book, it turned brown? Just like that, plain and simple, between your fingers. I'm already talking to you about my shit, because that's kind of what it's like to be sick. It would piss me off to die. There are still so many things to say, so many stories to tell. People who tell stories have no life. I always said I had to keep some stories to tell. Too late. I'm offloading everything.

"Maman, can you help me unwrap my present? I'm all thumbs."

I woke up my mother. I told her I was angry. WTF, no more cigarettes and no doughnuts? I don't know how to be in my body anymore. Should I take another blue pill to sleep? Or should I get up? I more often take one at night. I'm a special kind of vampire. The daylight gives me a headache. I'm on the couch, waiting. My new schedule: wake up at two in the morning, or at three or four. Sleep at seven. Sometimes I close my eyes for hours. I think about all kinds of things. *Drama Queens*, my next book. Life. How short it is. For me. I can't move with my walker forever. I'm going to have to go into the hospital. I can't ask people to adapt to my schedule.

"Maman, can you make me crepes this morning?"

I asked her. Fucking queen. Drama queen. I should make use of this time to write this morning. After an hour, I start to get a headache. Too late. Only good for eating crepes. Even that. It's not a pretty sight, watching me eat. My greatest fear almost came true yesterday in front of Daniel. I'm afraid of shitting myself when I get up, because of the momentum. It was just a little toot yesterday. I was the only one who knew. I went to the bathroom. I hid. I wanted to cry. I always want to cry. I come up with scenarios before I fall asleep. They're always tearjerkers. In all the scenarios, I am going into palliative care. End-of-life care. And I'm dying. Full of shit. In my diaper. Fuck, do I cry. Yesterday they delivered my wheelchair. A depressing visualization exercise. All because my mother isn't made of metal. I have to hold it together. To be a little solid. I can't trust my legs anymore. My body is a wreck. I'm finished. Nothing left in there. Daniel called me. He wanted to invite me out for a walk. No. I can't walk. You'd have to push me in my new wheelchair. I didn't tell him that. I waited till the man left. A little shot glass of tears. *Ding, ding,* Daniel was there. We watched a film about Hitchcock. Translated. I fell asleep. He did too.

"Maman, can you buy me diapers tomorrow? Neon diapers wouldn't be so bad. Purple ones that match my hair."

This morning I pissed in my diaper. This morning it's my birthday. I'm alive. I got up, pissing in my diaper, too much liquid to hold, after another horrible fragmented night, but alive.

"Maman, the stain on the arm of my robe is not chocolate, I smelled it. I need help to get it off. Bad arm, good arm."

On the couch. Still bathing in my own piss. I get to the bathroom. I shit, brushed my teeth, the whole process, but didn't piss. I kept that for the diaper. I'm twenty-four now. Yes. Yesterday it was my birthday. It's the fifteenth of April, it is going to be fifteen degrees, and I'm alive. I'm twenty-four years old and I'm pissing on the couch, listening to loud music. I massage my knees, listening to my dancer beats. Tonight I climbed the Saint-Joseph Oratory. To start another book. Move on to something else.

"Maman, can you buy some coloured paper? I want to print out everything I've written and throw myself into it."

Thinking isn't fun anymore. It needs to be fun again. Otherwise the same thing will happen for reading. Speaking of reading, François Blais sent me his new book, the one that hasn't come out yet. An exclusive for my birthday. He won an award for *Document 1* at the Gala. He sent us a bunch of photos of himself with stuff up his nose. Yesterday I asked Britney Speaks to bring over her camera. We took a bunch of photos of me in the bath with my dildo on my forehead. My pink dildo that matches my pink hair. Fucking unicorn. I'm up to Document 81 in Word. I still don't feel like I've said everything.

"Maman, François Blais is definitely the man of my life."

Says the girl who pisses in her diaper, talks about her shit, and does a photo shoot with a pink dildo. I woke up with a little headache around eleven thirty.

1. I took Tylenol.
2. I peed in my diaper.
3. I put on my pink sweater.
4. I got to the living room without falling down, like a big girl.
5. I'm still going to have to wake up my mother so she can bring me my blue pill. Fail.

In any case, my mother thinks I shouldn't be having strokes of genius at night. She's worried about my fragmented sleep cycles. I sleep badly. The boar keeps running in circles.

"Maman, I don't want you to worry. I want you to be happy. To go to the movies with chivalrous gentlemen who take good care of you."

1. I pissed in my new beige night diaper.
2. It's seven thirty-eight in the morning and I just ate some cereal.
3. I have a little black dress.
4. I'm drinking coffee with chocolate milk.

Alice helped me with all that. There's the chains, right there. She always helps me. I always need help. I would be alone without her in my life. Best mother in the world.

"Maman, you're beautiful when you cry at the end of sappy movies. You're beautiful all the time."

The Breakfast Tub

A JOHN HUGHES FILM

Britney Speaks helps Victoria Love
into the bath. She sits next to the tub on a
brown cushion. Gifts for nursing friends.
Right in the eyes: this memory. Victoria
is eating leftover sushi. Britney Speaks:
"I heard they put arsenic in some kinds of
rice to make it white." Victoria Love: "I just
pissed in the tub as I was looking you right in
the eyes." The colour of the cushion
is important.

THE END

All of it filmed by Maggie Books, until this appears on the screen: "The young girl has stopped responding. Please restart the young girl."

Zizi, Empress of Austria

Last room of our exhibition. It's already over. Against the back wall, a giant hand giving the finger.

The finger is papier mâché, made of rental agreements.

A beautiful booger on the tip of the middle finger.

I was in Syracuse, New York. Without a gun. Sitting on a bench right in front of our hotel. With my big white fur hat, Marlboros, and coffee. Still in pyjamas. I needed to take a shit but I didn't want to disturb my friends with trumpet sounds in the bathroom. I lit another cigarette, I took another sip of coffee. I tried to forget. My nose was running, my pussy was dripping. This was a crazy, exciting day. I was going to the zoo. I was going to see my first real live fennec foxes at the Rosamond Gifford Zoo. I would have liked to stay in Syracuse forever. At the hotel forever. Nobody knew me there. I was just a girl. A girl you could point your gun at. I'm afraid of guns. We were in the States. There are guns everywhere there. I hadn't seen one yet. There would maybe be one at the zoo. In a holster on a belt. Or in a cage with the fennecs, as a toy. Guns freak me out. I wanted to forget that too. Cigarette, sip. Splash on the bench. I was perched on the bench like a hen. There were fireflies on the park benches. The girl at the front desk thought it was cute too. We talked about it. She thought everything was cute. It was so cute that my friends brought me to see the fennecs. She told me they were in the inside part of the zoo. She also told me it was the hotel manager who had made the little carrot muffins and raspberry scones. I took one to respect the stage directions. She looked at me. I wondered if she maybe had a gun on her. Maybe she was a security girl and it was mandatory. I took a muffin, a sip of coffee, and I went outside smiling. Get away from the belt. I went over to the bench, the closest one, the one where I was sitting with my back to the hotel. Forget her gun. Forget all the guns. Light another cigarette. All out of sorts. It'd be fine after a few puffs. I was lucky. The world loved me. It had told me so. My friends were sleeping. The muffin was in my stomach with the coffee. *Knock, knock.* I think it had done me good. I thought how I would thank the manager if I saw him. He wouldn't be afraid of me. He would think: "That girl doesn't have a gun, that girl is nice, she ate my tiny little muffin, she liked it and told me so. It's a bit much though that she's still in her pyjamas. I'll keep my hand on my belt. Just in case." Yellow buses pass. Children keep going to school. In English. With belts flying everywhere. With belts that tie everything and nothing together. Everything is going to be all right. Everything in its right place. Radiohead is dead. So are all those innocent children in Connecticut. So is Marie-Soleil Tougas, so is Ève Cournoyer. But not me. Not yet. Not for a while, I hope. Sip, cigarette. I feel like taking photos of everything, documenting everything. Instagramming this moment spent writing and smoking way too many cigarettes in Syracuse, New York, in pyjamas on a park bench that glows in the dark. With this coffee. This really good coffee. Thank you, manager. Maybe he picked the beans himself, made this coffee by the sweat of his brow, literally. I'll go get another in the lobby, go up to the room, shit, and get dressed. Play by play.

Somewhere on the Internet: a ton of photos of fennecs. Two fennecs in one enclosure, and Zizi, the lead fennec, in a separate enclosure. Definitely as punishment. Hunting and fishing are not for girls. Chainsaws, motorcycles, tattoos of skulls with flames: not for girls. Girls get brooches, diamonds, jewels. Signs that say, *You are a princess, my darling.* Zizi is. Zizi even became empress of Austria. Little girl crying as she scratches at the glass of the enclosure. Drama queen. I transpose myself. I am Zizi and I'm checking out the fennec through the glass. I name him Frank. He's my Prince Charming. There are still three fennecs. The universe likes a triangle. The other fennec with Frank is Hélène. Her ego is a bit bruised. In her red lighting. Buffet lighting. The corner for sulking. But the fennecs have real names. There's one named Pumpkin. It's written at the entrance to the zoo. Pumpkin. It reminds me of the pumpkin marmalade waiting for me in the fridge in Montreal. I need to taste it. I need to make Pillsbury Turnovers with it. It reminds me of the fennecs' faces. They will all be pumpkin-flavoured. I could ask my mother to make them for my funeral. I want my friends to eat well. I want happiness for other people. I want them to scatter my ashes in the bay at the family home in Kenogami Lake. It reminds me of the Austrian landscape. My mother and I are watching the *Sissi* trilogy. I put the first film on pause. That's how and where I want to be scattered. I did say *first film* and *pause*. You haven't heard the last of me. I'm a Victoria's Secret angel. In the corner of your apartment. Watching you jerk off.

Translator's Note

I was able to complete the first draft of my translation of *Drama Queens* during a month-long residency at the Collège International des Traducteurs Littéraires in Arles. I am very grateful to the wonderful people at ATLAS for this precious time and space to work, and to my brilliant fellow residents for their conversation and company.

A special thanks is due to Aleshia Jensen for her close reading of this translation and invaluable suggestions and ideas, and to Caroline Marinacci and Luke Major for helping me unravel and understand some of Gendreau's references.

It has been an honour and a thrill to be a part of bringing Gendreau's œuvre into English, and I am grateful to the people who share in this work and make it possible: thank you to Éric de Larochellière of Le Quartanier and Mathieu Arsenault for their support and their assistance along the way, and to Jay MillAr and Hazel Millar for the thoughtful consideration they have put into publishing Vickie Gendreau, the great writer, in English.

—Aimee Wall

Colophon

Manufactured as the first English edition of *Drama Queens* in the fall of 2019 by Book*hug Press.

Copy edited by Stuart Ross.
Type + design by Malcolm Sutton.

bookhugpress.ca

Book*hug Press